The
TAF
Omnibus

Triangle Association of Freelancers

(Stories & Poems)

Arlene S. Bice
Contributing Editor

Cover Design by James, GoOnWrite.com

Arlene S. Bice, Contributing Editor

Dedication

This book is dedicated to our faithful readers and to our brave writers who parted from their usual genres to stretch their imaginations and create interesting, suspenseful, loving, or humorous stories, and poetry for you.

Additional TAF Publications

A Taste of Taffy: Samplings from Triangle Area
                    Freelancers
TAF Stays Home: 29 Freelancers Writing
The TAF Reader: Books on a Freelance Writer's Shelf

"To survive, you must tell stories."
--Umberto Eco

About TAF

Triangle Association of Freelancers (TAF) is a writers' organization founded by Don Vaughan. Our members can be in touch daily, available by email. If you are a novice writer stumbling over a problem, ask and you will receive multiple thoughts and opinions on the subject. When experienced writers have a thought that may help a member, it will appear in the TAF thread for any member who may benefit. Support and advice is always for the asking. A shared "Bravo" or equivalent appears for successes and words of compassion for any disappointments. Laughter gets tucked in between to keep us uplifted.

We are a writing family that began in the Raleigh (NC) area in 2003. From there we've progressed to non-profit status while growing members from across the country, yet kept the intimacy of hometown. Our first, annual WRITE NOW! conference opened its welcoming arms in 2008 with in-person conferences each year following until COVID-19 closed personal contact in 2020. This year, we successfully returned to our in-person conference.

When our actual meetings and conferences were denied us, Don created and moderated TAF Talks. This series of informative, lively conversations with impressive, high-profiled, professional writers, and editors is conducted by Zoom. Members are able to ask questions and interact with our guests.

Our monthly meetings continued, now virtual, usually with an interesting guest onboard. Members have offered additional helpful information by conducting virtual mini workshops. We network, share leads on job opportunities and markets; at times reveal personal experiences in business, good or bad. Our members represent all areas of the writing industry; publishers, formatters, editors, coaches, consultants, etc. Many of our writers of various genres are multi-published and award-winning.

Often, as with our anthologies and this omnibus, we open the way for a writer to be published, adding to the resume` they are building.

 Please visit our website: https://tafnc.com

Arlene S. Bice
Contributing Editor

Introduction

Stories. I was lucky enough as a youth to experience the story telling around the campfire after hunting season ended and the hunters cooked venison for us families. We were surrounded by deep darkness in the pine forests of New Jersey that intensified the teller's story. As the night went on I sat enrapt, eyes glued to the voice, my imagination growing by the minute. As the adults consumed more beer, the stories got wilder and louder. But the evening always ended with guitars strumming and singing to send us youngsters off to bed with happy endings. Hence the writer already within me, marinated.

Stories. My brother Bob and I sat on the carpeted floor, glued to the voice from the big radio that stood tall in our cozy living room. We anticipated the buzzing sound that introduced *The Green Hornet,* or a deep voice announcing *The Shadow Knows,* or *Inner Sanctum* that came with the squeaky door. It warned us what was coming next. We loved stories of all kinds from library books to comic books (called graphic novels today) we traded with friends.

Fiction. Many of our members are writers of non-fiction for magazines, journals, blogs, and various publications that call for interviews, articles about parenting, health, animals, local events, etcetera, and books of memoir, poetry, essays, history, etc. But sometimes in the back of the mind smolders a challenge to write a fictional story, to stretch the imagination and see what comes. It teases until an opportunity arises.

Gathered here are 18 members who stepped outside their familiar creative zone to stretch their imaginations and to expand their writing skills. They answered the call of opportunity. Writing fiction is different. Creating memorable characters, good or bad, breathing life into settings the reader can visualize is the enticement. Add having a plot that intrigues, catches your attention and holds it. Writing fiction is definitely different.

Here we offer you a wide selection of stories and poetry to suit your mood and exercise your mind and heart. Enjoy the stories TAF members have penned for you, the reader.

Arlene S. Bice
Contributing Editor

Contents

Lauren Clemmons is a published author based in Raleigh, North Carolina. Her essays, poetry, and fiction appear in anthologies, including TAF publications.

Time Warp

Carl slumped nonchalantly in his desk, more in the manner of a stylish, bored executive than in the manner of a rebellious student. His nonchalance was characteristic of his attitude toward himself. He had always considered himself a polite, yet direct person who knew where he was going and when he would get there. The only problem, it seemed, with his life was time. There was too much of it and it moved quickly, but not quickly enough. Time was in his way.

Although the days went by fast, there were so many more that he had to wait for and to live through. Today, he thought, was a day like any other school day, the kind that came and then faded without notice, the kind which caused him to wonder whether or not it had really been there. He had thought enough about reality and imagination in conjunction with time to the point where he wondered what really existed and what did not. Sometime he even wondered if his thoughts were real or imaginary, existent or nonexistent. He was puzzled but he had a solution. He knew that it would be futile to ponder the problem, especially if he really did not exist in the first place, so he concluded that time was irrelevant. His only hope was for his eighteenth birthday because, contrary to popular scientific belief, that year was the true ending of the gestation period of the human being. Until then, Carl wrote off time as being one of life's deceptions and left the matter at that.

Carl straightened from his slump as Mr. Hadley came bumbling into the classroom in his usual, fast-paced duck walk. Hadley, or Dave, as the students had informally christened him, was likeable but only partially respected. His thick-lensed glasses coupled with the disheveled brown hair on his balding head lent themselves to the look not of intellect, but of absent-mindedness. On several occasions, when Hadley was busy grading papers, Carl had discreetly studied the flurry of Hadley's motions. The jerkiness of the left hand holding a pen and the scratching marks on the paper conflicted with the syncopated tapping of his right foot on the floor and his right hand on the desk in between a background of sighs, sniffles, and occasional pencil-gnawing. Carl figured that Hadley's lack of bodily control demonstrated an inner sense of extreme conflict and tension.

For some reason, Carl wanted to attribute Hadley's oddities to those thick-lensed glasses, but Carl did not know exactly what he could, or should, infer. Carl himself had often tried to look beyond the barrier of the glasses to see if he could amass any thoughts or motives stirring like trapped butterflies in a jar. After careful peering and squinting, Carl deduced from his intense, analytical observation that Hadley had the beadiest eyes that he had ever seen and if a thought did reside in Hadley, it was held back by those two vacuums of prescribed glass.

Hadley stood, his back to the class, and made a mark on the chalkboard. He slowly rotated and faced the class. Hadley had the most bizarre-looking grin on his fact that Carl thought was fiendishly possible. "Class," said Hadley in his famed matronly tone, "Class, this is a dot."

"No kiddin' Sherlock!" mouthed an obnoxious guy in the back row.

Hadley smiled again, in a curt sort of way, and then continued. "This is a dot. For your assignment today, class,

you are to write a creative story. You are to describe the dot
and the circumstances of its existence by answering the
questions: who, what, when, where, why and how."

The obnoxious guy in the back of the class groaned.
The boy seated across from Carl and hunched over with his
head on his desk obviously did not hear Hadley because he
continued to snore. The petite girl in front of Carl rallied to
the assignment as if it were a cry to right the wrongs of the
world. She nibbled at her pencil, scribbling down famous
phrases in between clamps. The remaining members of the
class, the unthinking mob that they were, methodically drew
out paper and pens and began the torturous miracle of
transporting words from the brain to the paper along a transit
system of nerves, veins, pores, and pens.

The only exception was Harmony, who rhythmically twisted
her long brown ponytail around and around the middle finger
of her right hand. It was a mesmerizing motion. Carl
suddenly longed to touch the ponytail himself. He wanted to
breathe in the scent of her "Gee-Your-Hair-Smells-Terrific"
washed hair. All the popular girls in 9th grade were using
the shampoo. Once, and only once, Carl had been close
enough to Harmony to whiff her scented ponytail. It had
been a random timing of events. Carl was uncharacteristic-
ally running late to Hadley's class. Harmony was, as usual,
destined to arrive in Hadley's class mere seconds before the
tardy bell on account of her participation in the daily
popular-girl-meet-up between 7th and 8th periods. That day,
in his effort to beat the tardy bell, Carl ran the last twenty
steps to the classroom door and found himself literally on
Harmony's heels as they passed through the threshold. He
had been able to breathe in her scented pony-tail as they
crossed the threshold together followed by the tardy bell
clang. The fragrance immediately calmed him and erased his

13

tardy bell anxiety. The moment etched itself in his mind as his only, and therefore, best experience in getting close to a popular girl.

As he watched Harmony twist her ponytail around and around, it occurred to Carl that Harmony was discretely giving Hadley the "middle finger." Carl dismissed the thought. That just was not something a sophisticated popular girl like Harmony would do.

There was something, however, about the middle-finger twisting the ponytail that triggered Carl to come to the true realization of Hadley's being. Hadley was not absent-minded or even stupid. Hadley was crazy! How in the world could he, Carl, write intelligently, or even stupidly for that matter, about a yellow dot of chalk on the board? The idea was absurd, ridiculous! Something must be done to stop Hadley.

Then it occurred to Carl that these events were not real. Time was playing tricks again, deceiving him into thinking he existed when he really didn't. Carl looked over the petite girl's shoulder. She was writing something about a dot…no, a balloon and a girl at a fair. "It was the balloon of love."

Oh brother, thought Carl, had that girl actually written that? He glanced at the dot on the blackboard. The blackboard had always reminded him of a dark, dusky night. He liked walking at night along the road to his house because the night gave him the feeling of peace sublimed with horror. This juxtaposition of feelings sufficiently provided him with the high of an adrenaline rush.

As he walked down the road in his imagination, he began to feel different, yes, almost like another person. In his mind, Carl became another person. The person that Carl had become was commissioned X-7 and he was uniformed in a shiny, metallic suit typical of those worn in the 25th

14

Century. He was walking along a road on a grassy hillside. The night air was still and silent.

X-7 was not alone. K-7 walked in-step beside him. X-7 placed his arm around K-7's shoulder and hugged her closer to him as they walked. He loved her long brown hair. It shined like glass, even in the dark night. X-7 often found random strands of K-7's hair clinging to his metallic shirt sleeves after they had been together. He took it as a sign that they would be together forever.

Playfully, he ran his hand down the length K-7's long brown ponytail, giving it a gentle twist as he reached its end. X-7 felt a rush of intense comfort from the flowery scent of her hair which wafted through the still night air like a drifting, downy feather. K-7 smiled.

They were so perfect for each other. Of course, they were. They had been specifically matched for each other. The Universal Movement Against Uncertainty had resulted in numerous scientific and cultural advances, but in X-7's opinion, eliminating the uncertainty of finding the person to whom you would be matched during mid-years training was one of the most progressive and efficient outcomes of the Movement. X-7's and K-7's genetic regrouping neurology process took place in an encapsulated lab closet at their doctor's office. The process had been painless. After it was over, he and K-7 were matched. All uncertainties and incompatibilities were eliminated.

The painlessness of the process stood in stark contrast to the past. X-7 had read ancient literature about the angst, rejection, and turmoil involved in the ancient people-matching process for his age-group. Particularly horrifying and revolting to X-7 were the tales of the "popular girls" and the boys who longed to be near these girls, but were either not "seen" by these girls, or worse, taunted and

15

rejected. X-7 was so thankful he had never had such an experience. He really couldn't imagine it.

X-7 and K-7 continued their walk. After a short time, they reached K-7's home-base. K-7 and X-7 stood at the threshold of the concrete structure. They grasped hands fondly and warmly. Then it was time. X-7 and K-7 simultaneously pressed the release nodules on the forearm dashboards of their respective metallic-suits causing K-7 to disappear into the concrete structure and leaving X-7 alone on the road.

K-7's release-departure always felt unsettling to X-7. He knew this feeling was wrong. The release-departure was intended to be seamless and comfortable. X-7 suspected that an error had occurred during his genetic regrouping neurology process. X-7 was unsure how to handle his suspicion. How would the problem be fixed? He had the heart-hurting thought that the only way to correct the error would be to de-match him from K-7. He really couldn't imagine it. It was during these brief moments that X-7 glimpsed the darker reality. The Universal Movement Against Uncertainty had not succeeded in eliminating all uncertainty,

Now alone, X-7 continued walking along the road on the grassy hillside. The night air remained still and silent. Any other time after K-7 left him, X-7 gave little notice to the black canopy overhead, but tonight was different. He could feel it.

X-7 sat down on the wet grass. His gaze was fixed intently on a small fluorescent dot in the sky. It glowed dimly, yet it became brighter and brighter as it neared the planet. The dot-shaped object was no larger than the eraser tip of a pencil. It seemed to X-7 that it had shrunk in size since he had first seen it several miles away.

X-7's ears were soon stimulated by a faint whining sound being emitted from the dot-shaped object. What he thought had been a 3-dimensional sphere descending from the sky, was now a chalky-looking substance with only one dimension, as if it had been drawn on a blackboard and sent hurling into space.

Within seconds, the dot hovered precariously in front of X-7's eyes. It seemed to tempt him to swing out at it as if it were a pesky fly. Yet, like a fly, every time X-7 swung, the dot dodged the blow. The whining sound increased. X-7 was very annoyed. Why wouldn't it leave him alone? In a final attempt to rid himself of the dot, X-7 flung his arm wildly at it. Instantaneously, he felt a sharp stinging pain on his hand.

There, on his hand was the dot, no longer glowing or whining. Instead, all that was left of the dot was a whitish-yellow, chalky mark on his palm, as if he had been writing with chalk. Whatever the dot-shaped object was, it was destroyed.

The night atmosphere was again calm and silent as X-7 walked away, brushing chalk dust from his palm onto his pant leg. It was then that he saw a strand of K-7's long brown hair shimmering against his metallic sleeve— reminding him they would be together forever. He smiled.

Suddenly a burst of sound hit the air and Carl jerked up in his seat. The night sky and the road of Carl's imagination had faded. "Carl," proceeded Mr. Hadley, "will you please read the story you've written to the class?" Carl looked at the boy beside him who was still snoring in a low, wheezy, whining sound.

"No Carl, I'm not talking to Sleeping Beauty, I'm talking to you. Now read us your story."

Carl fidgeted. He could feel the redness of his face and his hands felt as wet as if the maintenance man in his body had turned on the water in order to prevent the blush of fire in his cheeks from spreading to another part of his body. "I'm sorry, but I haven't written one," replied Carl.

"Very well. You'll take a zero. Maybe you should try putting those daydreams of yours to work by writing stories about them," retorted Hadley.

Carl was amazed, not exactly at the zero, but at himself. He had never before allowed his daydreams to interfere with his school work. But something told him that he had not had an ordinary daydream. Had his daydream been real? For that moment in time, had he really been X-7? Was K-7 real? Strangely, the sudden thought of her ached his heart.

Just as Hadley gave Carl the verbal "zero," Harmony began twisting her long brown ponytail with her right middle finger. As she did so, she shifted side-ways in her desk chair toward Carl just enough that Carl could have sworn she looked at him and smiled. Did that just happen?

Hadley's chatter interrupted Carl's thoughts. He was saying something infamous about "using your time wisely," and then he addressed the petite girl sitting in front of Carl, asking her to read her story. She began in her monotonous voice, "The dot is a balloon of love given to the girl by her drunken but well-meaning father."

Carl sighed, slumping nonchalantly in his desk as he wiped his sweaty hands off onto his jeans. He did not notice the chalk smudge on his pant leg or the strand of long brown hair on his shirt sleeve.

Lauren Clemmons

18

Marvis Henderson-Daye has published her debut novel, *Nine Lives* and a nonfiction ebook, *Every Storm Runs out of Rain*. She is CEO of M. E. Henderson, Inc. where she uses urban line dancing to create a healthy community. She is a member of Triangle Association of Freelancers.

Imprint

Detective Sanchez thought that I wasn't listening to him. He couldn't see that I was in shock!

He reminded me, "Ms. Terry, you didn't answer my question!"

In my head, I was screaming, "I can't answer your question!" To him, I whispered, "I am not sure."

He continued, "Did your sister discuss any of her problems with you?"

Although I wanted to answer him truthfully, my family warned me about sharing my suspicions. When I told them that I thought she was murdered, they said that's your grief talking. Yet, I didn't believe that my sister had killed herself. Sure, my 30 years old sister faced life-altering challenges, but I didn't think she killed herself because of them. Or would they?

Detective Sanchez's tone brought me out of my thoughts, "Ms. Terry, I have waited patiently for your answers. I need to ask you these questions, which are routine for suicides."

Instead of answering him, I wanted to slap him. I wanted to scream, "My sister was a strong black woman that loved life. She would never kill herself!" I kept my mouth closed because I did not have any proof. So, I meekly answered, "When she won the beauty pageant, her life

19

changed." Before he asked me another question, I finished
our conversation, "While I suspected some of the changes
were not good, she didn't elaborate when the family pushed
for answers. If you will excuse me, I told my parents I would
meet them later."

The detective stood, "I am sorry for your loss. I will
complete my report in the next few days. The coroner's
report should also be completed in the next few days. Again,
I'm sorry." I stood and opened my sister's apartment door.
He turned around and handed me his business card, "If you
think of anything or need to talk, you can call me."

I mumbled, "Thanks."
As I shut the door, I turned to face the empty apartment. In
less than twelve hours, my family's lives changed forever.
My daddy's call at 5 am began the nightmare.

I heard daddy crying when I answered the phone,
"Pudding, this is daddy…I got bad news…"

I interrupted him, "Has something happened to
mom?"

He continued to whimper, "No, baby…It's your
sister, Chevy…She's gone…" Although I couldn't see him, I
heard his sobs. As the analytic child, I processed the
information while he gained his composure. When I didn't
hear the crying, I whispered, "What happened?"

As her emergency contact, NYPD contacted my parents with
the devastating news that my sister had committed suicide by
jumping from her apartment balcony. As the next of kin,
they flew to NYC for the awful task of identifying her body.
While my parents and siblings live in Pennsylvania, I live in
Virginia. Since I could not get a flight until noon, my task
was to secure her apartment. Once I landed, I dropped my
bags off at the hotel room that my parents reserved for my
other sister and me. My parents and that sister were making

arrangements at the local funeral home to transport her body to Pennsylvania.

Before my flight, my cell phone rang incessantly. During each call, I voiced my doubts about suicide. While some family members indulged in my hypothesis, others told me to accept it. It was my grief talking. No one wanted to discuss that we knew Chevy was keeping secrets from us. If we acknowledge that we knew she had secrets, were we responsible for her death?

As I walked through her apartment, my mind wandered. I discouraged her when she decided to enter the Miss USA Pageant. Regretfully, I wish her life had changed for the better when she won the pageant. Although she shared some problems, I knew she deliberately omitted others. I knew Chevy kept those secrets to protect us. She was the level-headed, seeing-the-glass-full daughter. I am the reactionary, take-prisoners daughter. My sister, Crystal, is the ride-or-die and you-are-guilty-until-proven innocent daughter.

How could a person who always saw the glass as full commit suicide? So, I didn't believe that she had killed herself. Unfortunately, if I could prove she was murdered, the damage to her reputation was done. People would always remember her as the beauty queen who committed suicide.

As I shook away the sadness that threatened to cripple me, I surveyed my sis' apartment. When I arrived, as the policemen were leaving, Detective Sanchez remained. Based on the condition of the apartment, their visit was short. The sadness threatened to overtake me again as I looked at the plywood covering the balcony window. I fought back hysteria as I remembered me joking about her need for a balcony.

"Why the hell do you need a balcony on the 19th floor? To catch pigeons for dinner?" I joked.

"Girl, I don't need my meat that fresh. My balcony gives me more natural light!" she insisted. Now, that balcony pierced a hole in my heart, so I turned away to take pictures to inventory her apartment. As I walked around the apartment, I wondered, "Why would a suicidal person wash all the dishes and put them in the cabinets and drawers?" Not a spoon, fork, or glass was out of place. The pots, pans, bowls, and plates were neatly stacked in the kitchen cabinets.

Curious, I opened the TV cabinet. Her CDs and DVDs were neatly arranged alphabetically in baskets. Shampoos, conditioners, makeup, and other toiletries were neatly arranged in her bathroom cabinets. Even the toilet paper was neatly stored in a lower cabinet. I became frantic as I opened the apartment's drawers, cabinets, and closets.

Not a single pair of shoes, dress, coat, or hat was out of place. The floors were almost spotless. Although my sister was the neat freak in the family, if she killed herself, why would she clean up her apartment? When I first noticed the faint acidic smell of bleach, I thought it was the chemicals that the police used before I arrived at the apartment.

The spotless home made my mind race because I knew my sister. If she were in danger, she would leave clues. So, my mission changed from inventory to investigation. I reopened every drawer carefully because I didn't want to disturb any evidence. My search seemed futile, and I was resigned to accepting that my sister may have killed herself. Before my family could call and ask about my progress with the inventory, I took pictures.

I felt like I was violating my sister's privacy when I entered her bedroom. I stalled when I opened her jewelry box. I made it in my middle school woodshop class. It looked like a child's attempt to make art with the burnt flowers and swirls of burnt wood. Every time I saw it on her dresser at home, in her dorm room, and her first apartment, I gave her permission to get rid of it. She would chastise me every time, "It's beautiful, and I love it!"

Once I got the courage to open the box, I was astonished to see her locket! She loved that locket as much as she loved the jewelry box. The sterling silver jewelry was etched with intertwined flowers and leaves on the front and smooth on the back. It was my grandmother's high school graduation gift. All the female family members received lockets that were the same size with similar chains, but the outside patterns were distinctly different. In each locket, my grandmother always placed two pictures of our family, the serious Terrys and the silly Terrys. Self-consciously, I reached into my shirt and caressed my locket. I always wore my locket when I headed into life's battle, and that day was a time to wear it.

Since my grandmother gave us pictures of the prior year's family, I was curious to see my sister's pictures. As I snapped the clasp to open the locket, I gave a deep sigh because the locket represented happier times in our lives. While it comforted us, I wondered if my locket would help me survive this tragedy.

When I opened the locket, I noticed the silly Terrys' picture. Instead of the serious Terrys' picture, there was a small disc that was the size of a fingernail. As I started to touch it, I snatched my fingers away. Could that be the clue that I was searching for? I quickly shut the locket. While I was excited, I was frightened because my hunch meant my sister was speaking to me from her grave. She knew the family would dispatch me to conduct the inventory, and I wouldn't believe she had committed suicide.

I almost tripped as I raced out of the bedroom. I couldn't remember where I put Detective Sanchez's business card. While I was excited about the disc, I was apprehensive about Detective Sanchez's reaction. If he dismissed me, what would I do? Since my sister put the disc in the locket, I took the chance and called him. I found the card and dialed the number. The phone rang two times.

He answered, "Good Afternoon, Detective Sanchez."

"Detective Sanchez, this is Chevy Terry's sister," I waited for his reply.

His voice softened, "Yes, Ms. Terry. How may I help you?"

My heart was racing as I answered, "As I conducted the inventory of my sister's apartment, I saw her locket in her jewelry box."

I heard him sigh as he answered, "Is that strange?"

I took a deep breath, "My sister cherished her locket. If she was going to kill herself, I don't think she would leave the locket."

"Well, if she was depressed…"

I fought the urge to curse, "There is something else. I found a small disc in the locket."

"Oh." I waited for him to continue. "How big is the disc?"

"About the size of a fingernail."

"Oh," he repeated. "Listen, Ms. Terry, I understand that you think your sister was murdered. But I didn't see any evidence of suspicious activity."

"Suppose the evidence is on the disc?" I questioned. When he didn't respond, I gave up, "I am sorry to bother you, thanks."

"Wait, Ms. Terry! How long will you be at your sister's apartment?

"I am waiting for my family to call. But I don't want them to know I'm still suspicious."

"I'm on the way."

My nervous energy caused me to jump with every noise. Because my sister's tragic end was broadcasted on every local and national station, I cut it off. So, when the ice cube hit the other ice cubes in the freezer, I almost fell off the stool. As I waited, I became paranoid and thought someone was watching me from hidden cameras.

When the doorbell rang, I opened the door before the second chime. Detective Sanchez seemed momentarily surprised. When I waited for him to walk in and didn't move, he sensed my fear because he guided me to the sofa.

Once I was seated, he sat in the occasional chair. He stated, "I am sorry that you and your family are suffering. So, the sooner we get some answers, the sooner you can grieve."

I nodded. When he held out his hand, I dropped the locket in his hand. As he opened the locket, I took a much-needed breath. He examined the inside without touching the disc. When he reached into his pocket, I almost screamed. Again, he sensed my fear by quickly removing his hand and explaining. "I brought my kit with tweezers in it. I don't want to damage the disc when I remove it."

I answered, "Okay. I am sorry that I'm skittish. It's just…" I couldn't finish my thoughts.

He responded, "No problem. You're taking a great risk asking for my help. If someone murdered your sister, you don't know who to trust. So, shall we see if this disc can help us?"

I nodded because the waves of emotions flooded my vision and voice. My fear over my safety, anger over my loss, and relief that my sister left clues were battling inside me. Although I could not bring her back, I needed the courage to discover what had happened.

I didn't flinch when Detective Sanchez reached into his pocket and withdrew a metal container the size of a deck of cards. I watched as he popped the container's latch, and an array of small tools was neatly arranged. Although his fingers seemed too big to grab the tools, his fingers were quite nimble. Once he grabbed the tweezers, he hunched over the coffee table that anchored the sofa and occasional chair. My curiosity overtook my fear, and I moved toward the coffee table. I watched as he lifted the disc from the locket.

While he inspected the disc, we were silent. When the inspection was completed, he sat the tweezers and the disc on top of the opened locket. We both shifted away from the table as if we were dancing together. He broke the silence, "The disc is a phone's SD card." I nodded. He continued, "Fortunately, I have the same phone. I wanted to take this minute so you can prepare yourself for what we may discover. Ready?" I nodded again.

Once he reached into his pocket and retrieved his phone, he grabbed another tool from his container. He used the tool to prick a tiny hole on the side of the phone. I was surprised when the storage compartment opened. With the tweezers, he removed his SD card from his phone, placed it on the locket, retrieved my sister's SD card, and placed it in his phone. With a quick snap, the SD card was secured in his phone. I didn't move as he booted his phone and punched his keypad as each screen popped up.

Still jumpy, I almost bolted when I heard the angry voice from his phone. The man with a southern drawl was shouting obscenities. While I wanted to grab the sofa's pillow to stifle my gasps, Detective Sanchez didn't appear to be fazed. The man's rant was based on his beliefs that the pageant was stolen from white women. Detective Sanchez explained as he stopped the obscenities-laced message,

"That was a voicemail from your sister's phone." He started another message, then another message, then another message...until he stopped the recordings. Although the voices were male and female, the message was the same. They threatened my sister's life because they were upset about her pageant success. Unbelievable!

Before I could rest, Detective Sanchez scrolled through his phone, and another recording started. I quickly realized that the recording was not a voicemail. When I heard my baby sister crying, I watched the video in horror.

"It's time for you to die," a person that wasn't visible screamed.

My sister pleaded, "Please just leave."

"We ain't leaving. No, we're going to create our own pageant. We are gonna help you fall to your death, so the true winner can take her rightful place." The video showed three menacing white men with intimidating scowls standing in my sister's apartment.

When my sister cried, one of the men told her to shut up because he saw those same tears when she stole the pageant. The other man told her that she didn't deserve to live. At that point, she ran to her bedroom and slammed the door. When she heard the scratching from her doorknob, she looked into the camera. I wanted to scream when I saw the terror on her face, her makeup smeared, and her hair plastered to her wet face. As the scratching turned into clicks, her face changed.

"I pray that my family understands that I didn't die intentionally. I didn't share my nightmarish life with them because I wanted to spare them, and I didn't want them harmed. I participated in the Miss USA pageant to use the money and the platform to better serve my community. My prayer is that my work and my life weren't in vain. I will miss you all terribly." After the last doorknob's click, my sister walked into her bathroom, washed her face, and smoothed her hair. The video stopped.

While Detective Sanchez looks for those murderers, I'm at the memorial listening to the beautiful tributes about my sister. Because it's an active case, my parents and siblings are the only ones who know the truth.

Unfortunately, by the time the perpetrators are caught and tried in court, my sister's reputation is damaged. While the world will know her as the Miss USA pageant winner who committed suicide, she'll be my sister who gave her life to help her community. As the soloist sang the spiritual, "If I Can Help Somebody," my tears flowed because my sister's imprint on the world won't be in vain.

Marvis Henderson-Daye

Chanah Wizenberg received her BA from Hunter College in English and Creative Writing. Her writing has appeared in several magazines and multiple anthologies. Chanah has been a professional ballerina, a pastry chef, and English teacher. She resides in Raleigh (NC) with her dog, Asha, and her cat, Marmalade.

The Betrayal of Sarah

It had started at breakfast, when she realized she was out of coffee. Coffee was a must; there was no functioning without it. That meant she would have to stop for some on her way to work, and THAT meant she'd be late. It would be the second time, and that meant another write-up in her file. There was already one; if she got a third one, she'd be fired.

Coffee. It made her think of her clients. They had their addictions, and she had hers. Sarah sighed, a big, down-into-her-toes sigh. At least a coffee addiction was socially acceptable. Every substance abuse counselor she knew was addicted to it.

When she finally arrived at work, she opened her calendar to preview her day. While grabbing her cup for that delectable first sip, a text labeled "urgent" pinged her phone. Well, that can't be good. She clicked on the text. Walter, the big boss: "In my office, right now." What the hell is that about? She texted back, "Coming," taking a big gulp of coffee. Mistake!! Too hot, burning her tongue and the roof of her mouth. Sarah almost choked, but got it down before hurrying off to see what Walter wanted, her mouth tingling, on fire with a weird numbness.

Seeing her at the door, Walter motioned her to enter. Standing behind his chair, wringing his hands, he said only, "Take a seat."

Although his voice sounded calm enough, Sarah was alarmed by his behavior —he only wrung his hands when super upset. "I'd rather stand." Sarah stood there in front of his desk, clutching the edges of her sweater. "What is it you want to see me about?"

"Sarah, you're one of our best counselors here at Hope Springs. I trust you, your methods, and ethics. It pains me to tell you there's been a complaint."

"A complaint?" Sarah could feel the color drain from her face. Where addicts are concerned, they go for the worst-case scenarios, the biggest drama, the ultimate of clusterfucks. She could feel the sweat under her arms.

"One of our patients has filed it. He claims you sexually assaulted him."

 Sarah would have laughed out loud, if Walter's face wasn't turning red. He was pacing now, too. "Walter, what the hell? You know I'd never do that, not ever."

"I know, but, but we have to investigate it. And what makes it worse is that he claims he has a witness to it."

"That's impossible! It never happened. Who's claiming this and who is the lying witness?"

"Todd Small is the one who put forth the complaint."

"That's the guy I had to dismiss as a patient. He wasn't making any progress, a total narcissist and he kept coming on to me. It's in all my notes. Have you read them?"

"Yes, I've read your notes; they're good and thorough."

"So, who's the so-called witness?"

"Um, I'm so sorry Sarah…it's Melonie."

"What?" She had to sit before her knees gave out, "Melonie Taylor?" Melonie was one of Sarah's closest friends at work. They'd been to each other's house. For Christ's sake, this couldn't be happening!

Rubbing his hands back and forth, and stuttering a little, Walter continued, "I'm…I'm…I'm af-afraid I have to suspend you for now, with pay, until we get this mess sorted out."

"Holy Christ, Walter!" It was all Sarah could do to hold back the tears, her breath coming in quick gasps, "Do I have to clear out m-my desk?"

"Oh, no, that won't be necessary, but you can't come back in until we resolve the problem. I'm so sorry," Walter finished, hanging his head now, hands gripping the back of his chair, his face gray.

Sarah, numb from the shock, her breath slowing, walked out of Walter's office. The news was surreal. She must have had a dissociative moment, because before she realized it, Sarah found herself back in her office. Robotically, she picked up her purse, her phone and coffee, and went home.

It was impossible to stay in the house. She had to get out before she suffocated. The walls were closing in, sucking the oxygen out of her lungs. Sarah knew this was just a reaction, the result of hearing that her best work friend had betrayed her. Todd Small and Melonie Swift out for her job. God knows why.

As she stood up from the couch where she'd been attempting to enjoy her coffee, she noticed, in a detached sort of way, that her mouth still felt awful — that same numbness she'd experienced earlier. "I've got to go for a walk." She headed out the door, shoving her phone into her back pocket as she went.

31

Starting along the garden path that led to the town woods behind her house, Sarah couldn't help thinking about her career choice. Addicts, good god, what possessed me to work with addicts? All they do is lie. She groaned. It was time to do some soul searching. Substance abuse counseling: a career that guaranteed early burnout. She had been so sure she would beat the odds. Started her first job right out of college at 21. It was the naïveté and arrogance of youth that made her believe she was different back then. But no, she wasn't different at all, just young and stupid like most people in their early twenties. Now she was 32, and already saw grey hairs showing up, along with an unsightly rash on her forearms that refused to go away, and tension headaches — lots of tension headaches.

But if she left, she wanted it to be her decision. I'll be damned if I let that sick fuck end my career or go to jail because of him…and her.

As she walked along, she started noticing the sweet aroma of the dome-topped white flowers of King Edward's yarrow, the deep scent of wild lavender, and the delicious fragrance of the lilac trees, her favorite. Focusing on their beauty, she forced herself to take in some deep breaths, holding each one before exhaling. After three of these, she could feel her body begin to relax. It was working; she was feeling grounded: a good feeling. Her pace slowed; she took in the sweet scents of the other plants on the property, including some Honey Perfume roses, with their delicious, spicy scent. All these fragrances blended into an earthy, Divine bouquet. She was lucky to have rented that small house, with such a delightful garden in back, leading to these calming woods. Perfection.

Soon, she approached the weather-worn back fence. As she lifted the latch and pushed open the gate, it squeaked in protest. It closed with a bang, the spring too tight, causing some birds to take sudden flight and grating on Sarah's already-frayed nerves. She jumped, startled and gasping for breath. Placing a hand over her heart, which hammered against her chest, she took a few more deep breaths to slow it down before continuing.

Picking her way along the rough trail, she headed for her favorite spot. The deeper she got, the cooler it became, thanks to the cover of the broad oaks and tall pines. The air smelled of pine, the earthy richness of decaying leaves, and other remnants of plants and trees. For a while, Sarah thought of nothing but these rich scents and sounds of the forest: not of the betrayal, just the birds calling to each other, the squirrels scampering up and down trees, and an owl hooting every few minutes. Hearing an owl surprised her. An owl in daylight? She thought owls only came out at night. She made a mental note to Google it when she got home. For now, she plodded along toward what she considered her private oasis. It wasn't hers, of course, but so far, she'd seen no one else there. In fact, she'd had the good fortune to not see any person out here at all. Very fortunate, indeed. She loved the idea of being the only one here, in her most favorite of places. Her own secret garden.

Just as she broke a sweat, despite the shade from the canopy of the trees, she arrived at her sanctuary. A little clearing, complete with a pond encircled by large rocks. Maybe they were small boulders. Sarah wasn't sure. There were several of them positioned around the pond, featuring fine, flat tops — perfect for sitting. There were two oak trees here, too. They had entwined around each other as they grew, and then fanned out, as if deciding they wished to be separated. Each one reaching away from the other and then changing their minds again, they'd grown back together, twisting around one another once more, taking a little dip in the center, as if to give a kiss before reaching up toward the sky. The open space, and the little dip before continuing their journey skyward, made the shape of a heart.

Sarah was just about to step around that tree when she heard something. She froze. Despite the hotness of the day, a chill ran through her body. Her heart skipped a beat. She instinctively held her breath and sweat began to soak her underarms. What was that? Surely no one was in her place of refuge? Oh god, of all days! There! There it was again. Sarah forced herself to exhale. It was no good: Her heart was charging like a racehorse, her whole body shaking. Someone, or multiple someones, were in her sanctuary. She was hearing subdued voices. Her fear transitioned to anger. Still hidden, she pulled out her cell phone and set it to video record whoever was there.

"Hey man, you got the stuff?" said some guy with a raspy voice.

"Yeah, I got it. You got the cash?"

That one sounded like a woman. The voice was familiar.

"This better be good shit, not that stuff with fentanyl in it."

"My stuff is all fentanyl free, pretty boy."

Oh my god, it's a drug deal! Just what I don't need! And with that realization, Sarah's fear transformed to rage. "Hey!" She shouted as she flew around the tree, "Get out! Take your goddam deal somewhere else!" She stood with right her hand balled up into a fist, the left clutching her phone, which she'd pulled from her pocket. Her chest was heaving, her face burning, her throat on fire from screaming at them. The effing losers!

"Sarah? What the fuck? Must you ruin everything?" Sarah stopped short, incredulous, "Melonie?"

Melonie's "client" turned around now. "You know this chick? What the hell she's doing here?" Looking back at his dealer, now, "You said no one came here. Give me my damn drugs and I'm outta here!" With that he grabbed for his bounty, but she grabbed his wrist and twisted it. "Pay me first or I'll break it."

"Ok, ok," he pulled out a wad of cash from his pocket and threw it at her feet. "Here! Now gimme." She let go of his wrist, shoved the drugs into his hand, and he took off.

"Now, what are you doing here?" Melonie demanded.

Shocked at her friend's — make that EX-friend's — behavior, Sarah collapsed onto the nearest rock, still breathing heavily. She needed some time, if only a few minutes, to get her wits together. She placed her phone next to her on the rock, out of view of Melonie. This day just went from bad to royal suckage.

"Better question," said Sarah, when Melonie had retrieved the cash her junkie had thrown down. "How did you find out about this place, and does this have anything to do with you and Todd? I mean, what the absolute fuck, Melonie?! I thought you were my best friend!"

Melonie seemed to deflate, and she sat down on the rock nearest to her, the anger drained out of her and launched right back into Sarah. "Answer me, asshole! If you're hell-bent on ruining my career, you'd better tell me the whole story."

Melonie sighed, "I'm sorry, Sarah, I..."

Sarah cut her off. "Bullshit! Save it for your patients, which you won't have for very long, once I tell Walter I caught you dealing! Your career will be over, and you'll have a new residence — in a cell."

"Oh, you don't have any proof. You always were a perfect little princess who could do no wrong; it's sickening. After you dumped Todd as your patient, I took him on and he wound up showing me a far more lucrative side hustle than selling that Legal Guard shit you got me involved in, turned out to be a freaking pyramid scheme."

"I'm not the one who got you into Legal Guard. You think selling drugs is better? You don't see the irony in that, do you? And keep telling yourself that I don't have proof. Go ahead. Now tell me why you lied and said you witnessed me making passes at Todd? I'd rather claw my eyes out than seduce that narcissistic schmuck."

"First, show me you me your so-called proof."

"No. You can trust I have it."

"If you had it, you'd show it to me, because you're such a freaking trusting naïve Pollyanna."

"I'm waiting," said Sarah in a low, quiet voice. If Melonie knew her, she'd know to be worried right now.

"I guess I owe you that much. It's like I said, when you dumped Todd, I took him on. You've got him all wrong. He's no narcissist. He's a kind, sensitive, and smart. And you have always been a stuck-up, know-it-all, look-at-me, I'm-perfect bitch."

How can I have misjudged this woman so much? She's a fucking psycho moron. "If you think that, why the hell did you stay friends with me all these years? I'll tell you one thing, you're a damn good actress. I never suspected, ever, that you felt that way."

Melonie continued, "I knew I had to be, that's why. Walter did me a favor by hiring me, and I had to make sure he believed he made the right decision. I had to stay. I needed this job. I got fired from my last counseling job and my only option was this one."

"Why would he do you a favor? That's not his thing," said Sarah, furrowing her brow. It made little sense. Walter never did favors and he sure as hell didn't hire people who had been fired from a substance abuse counseling job.

He wouldn't take the chance especially, knowing Melonie had just four years in her recovery. Not enough. Sarah wondered why he hired her. Melonie must have snowed him as badly as she'd snowed her into believing she was a smart, caring, compassionate counselor with a great sense of humor. Melonie's a goddam phenom.

"He's my uncle," Melonie smiled. "My daddy made him promise to give me a chance. Them being brothers and all, he had to honor his family."

Sarah jumped to her feet. "Your uncle?! No way!"

"Yep, good ol' Uncle Walter, he made me swear I wouldn't let anyone know we're related. I was never ever to call him Uncle. Now, I really must go," Melonie stood up to leave.

"Not so fast. You haven't told me why you said you were a witness to Todd's made-up story."

"Oh, that. I just wanted to see you fall. You're one of those people who gets everything handed to them on a fucking silver platter."

At this, Sarah burst out laughing. "Wow, you really are several bricks short of a full load, and I got everything about you wrong. My parents were addicts, died of an overdose after shooting up in the car with me and my brother in the backseat. Some old lady saw my folks passed out and called the cops. And that was it. My brother and I were split up and bounced around different foster homes until we aged out. I assume he aged out, but he could've been adopted. I've no idea. After that horrible day, I never saw him again. So no, not only was nothing ever handed to me, I worked my ass off to get where I am and I'm sure as hell not going to let you or Todd end my career."

"Yeah, right, look who's telling stories now," with that, Melonie stomped off, leaving Sarah to stew in her thoughts.

As she sat and stared into the greenish-blue water of the pond, a tear slipped down her cheek. Her private oasis had been sullied. She must find a way to make it pristine again. That meant getting Melonie out of her life and Todd as well. What a pair they turned out to be.

Wiping away the tear, she collected her thoughts. How could she nail these two? Killing was not in the equation, even though that was an immediate fantasy. I have got to have a plan. An airtight, solid plan. Drumming her fingers against the rock, she wracked her brain for a solution. Adjusting her hands behind her to lean on, while swinging her legs in frustration, her left hand landed on her phone.

The recording! She grabbed her phone and hit the green button to play it back. Nothing was there! She swiped and swiped, but it was gone or hadn't recorded at all! What the fuck! She was doomed. No recording, no evidence. "Dammit!"

Time for Plan B. Come on Sarah, think. Who do I know that could help me? She leaned forward, elbows on thighs, hands cupping her face. She starred into the pond in hopes it would reveal something to her. After what seemed like hours, Sarah had an epiphany. Edgar, Edgar might help me. One of our best success stories. Poor Edgar had arrived at the hospital, a hard-core case. The nurses had to lock away the alcohol pads so he wouldn't steal them and suck out the alcohol. He'd grown from that downtrodden, sick-as-hell soul, to graduating the program with a dream of having his own detective agency. And he'd done just that. Sarah had been his counselor. I'll call him, she thought. He told me if I ever needed anything, just call. The thought of him helping her made her smile.

Sarah pushed off the rock and flew down the path, homeward bound. As she ran through the woods, she remembered Lilith. Lilith was a genuine friend. She worked for the Playhouse downtown. She oversaw wardrobe, make-up, and hair for the actors, for film and theater productions. It'd be too early to call her for help with a disguise, so she could follow Melonie and moron. Lilith lived up to the meaning of her name, belonging to the night. Working for the Playhouse was perfect for her. It meant she could sleep until noon before reporting to work in the mid-afternoon. Sarah would call her around two. But now she must get home and call Edgar.

The adrenaline still rushing through her veins, Sarah careened through the back door, stumbling into the kitchen island. Sweating and panting, Sarah stayed where she landed, on her elbows with palms smacked down on the counter of the island and caught her breath. Man, was she thirsty! Thirsty and drenched with sweat. Ugh. She needed something cold to drink and a quick shower before she called Edgar. That would give her time to slow down, and to think through her plan.

Edgar came through, supplying some binoculars, a camera with long-range zoom capabilities, a backup camera and video camera, GPS tracker, and an audio amplifier. Best of all, Edgar was going to go with her and do the heavy lifting. What a guy. Next was Lilith. Sarah rang her up and filled her in on the news, "What a lowly cow! Count me in, Sarah! Come right down and we'll get you fixed up. By the time I'm done with you, no one will know it's you."

"You're a lifesaver, Lilith," said Sarah. "I'll be right there."

Three hours later, Sarah was unrecognizable. Lilith decked her out with a Lucille Ball-looking wig, a Taylor Swift nose, and some cat-eyed fake glasses. The make-up consisted of adding a beauty mark just below and to the right of her mouth, and another left of her eyebrow. Lilith used honey-white foundation to lighten Sarah's tanned complexion. Sarah's eye makeup was given a natural look, including lipstick — all chosen to homogenize her in a crowd. For clothing, she found a nondescript sundress. It was khaki and white with a layered look, rounded neck, and side pockets. Lilith found some beige sling-back sandals in her size. Then, to top it all off, a straw sunhat. The most popular kind of the season, so Sarah would blend in.

When Lilith learned Edgar was going to help run the show, she had to be part of it.

"Oh, let me come, Sarah! It'd be great to nail that frump dragon."

"Okay, you're in, and thanks for the transformation. It's fantastic. I don't even recognize myself," said Sarah.

Armed with their surveillance equipment, Sarah in full incognito garb, the three set off to complete their mission.

"Where to?" asked Edgar, after they'd piled into his nondescript grey Honda Accord.

"Well, it's almost 6:00. She should be finishing up at work. That is, if she went back after her drug deal," said Sarah.

"Okay," said Lilith, "let's start there. Do you know a good place where we can watch for her, on the down low?"

"Let me think while we head over there."

"Off we go then. In fact, I know a suitable spot," said Edgar, a smile playing on his lips.

"What?" Asked Sarah.

"Um, when I was contemplating getting treatment, there was a spot I liked to hangout and smoke while I watched the comings and goings of people."

"I can assume you weren't smoking cigarettes?" asked Sarah.

"You sure can," laughed Edgar. "Anyway, it's a perfect spot. There's a great big old oak tree and some bushes around it. The bushes help make the car blend in without blocking the view."

"Oh, I know where you're talking about. It's not too far from the food truck that comes at lunchtime. That's perfect. You can see everything from over there."

"I hope she's still there," said Lilith. "That'll make it so much easier to follow her."

They were in luck. Not five minutes after they pulled into the spot by the tree, Melonie came out the front door. She was parked at the other end of the lot. "Hey, look at that," remarked Sarah. "She's driving a Dodge Charger, and it's purple." Unable to help herself, she burst out laughing.

"I don't get it," Lilith responded. "What's so funny?"

"I think I know, Edgar chimed in, laughing along. "Didn't the Chevy company name that color 'Hellraisin'?"

"Yep," said Sarah, "like its tailor-made for Melonie's personality — hell-raisin' for sure. I hadn't made the connection before."

"Oh, now I get it: an aptly-named car and color, a true representation for that twat's character," said Lilith. "And look how sparkly it is in the direct sunlight, all glitter to blind you to who she really is underneath. Yep, it all fits. Who woulda thought how much a car can show someone's true personality?"

"Yep," said Sarah.

"Hey, based on that, Lilith, what does my car say about me?" asked Edgar.

"And me," said Sarah.

Giggling, Lilith responded, "Well, Edgar, you drive a boring car. It's a drab grey with tinted windows in the back, not even a sunroof. It blends in with hundreds of others on the road, just like it. I suppose you chose it after opening

41

your P.I. business. You need a car that doesn't stand out. It also suggests you are strait-laced and practical."

Sarah laughed out loud at this description. "On the nose, Lilith, well done!"

"What can I say?" said Edgar, a big shit-eating grin on his face. "You nailed it. Now, what about Sarah's car? What does it say about her?"

"Hmm, Sarah drives a yellow, make that a nitro yellow Chevy Spark. It's cute and little. Sarah's cute, but not so little." At this she shot a sideways glance at Sarah with a big smile and a wink. "She does have a bright personality. As for the nitro part, when needed, she sure has a spark of energy that catapults her forward, kind of like a driver using nitro when starting a race. Do ya see what I did there, spark? Her car's a Chevy Spark." With that, Lilith began to giggle.

Sarah loved her giggle. It put her in mind of a meandering brook, starting with a soft bubbling that transformed into a robust laugh, almost to a guffaw. "Well done, Lilith!" Sarah and Edgar both laughed, for Lilith's giggle-laugh was contagious.

"Hey, we've got movement," said Edgar.

"Stay back so she doesn't see us," said Sarah. Edgar gave her a side-eye look. "I am a P.I., I've got this."

"Sorry, Edgar, just nervous."

They drove the rest of the way in silence. Each one was contemplating where Melonie was headed and if she was going to meet up with anyone. It was important to get the evidence they needed. In what seemed like an eternity, but was only five minutes later…

"Look, it's that dive bar Lilith and I used to go to," said Sarah.

"Um, you went to a dive bar?" asked Edgar.

"Back in the day, Sarah was a wild woman," said Lilith, smirking at Sarah.

"Uh, no, not really. It was affordable. I was still in school, working on my bachelor's," said Sarah, staring holes into Lilith's brain. "Mind if we get back on track, you know, keep our focus?"

"Sure, kiddo, we've got you, don't we, Edgar?"

"Absolutely. So, Sarah, you want to be the one to seek and discover?"

"Damn right, I do. What equipment should I take?"

"I'll go with her," said Lilith. That way, I can do the talking when ordering — don't want to risk the evil queen recognizing her voice."

"Good idea. I brought earwigs for each of us. It's important I be able to hear what's going on, in case you need some help in there." Edgar gave Sarah and Lilith their earwigs, keeping one for himself. As they put them on, he continued, "Remember, I put an app on your phone with a boosted listening device that records. All you've got to do is open the app, Smart Listen, and then set the phone on the table. Make sure it's set up to go to the black screen within three seconds, so no one will see the open app. Lilith, you wear the camera pin, just attach it like any other pin or brooch you'd wear. Okay?"

"Got it," said Lilith.

"Me too," said Sarah.

"Off you go then, you two, I'll be listening. Good luck."

Once they were settled at a table where they could observe Melonie, Lilith flagged down a server. "We'd like two of whatever you have on tap and some pretzels, please."

"We've got Guinness and Miller Lite on draft. Which one do you want?"

"Guinness, please," said Lilith.

"Two Guinnies and a pretz," said the server as she hurried off to get them their order.

"Remember to nurse the beer as much as we can. We don't know how long we'll be here," Sarah said.

"Right, get your phone ready. I'm all set with my pin. Edgar turned it on before I got out of the car."

They didn't have to wait long. "Hey, look at that," murmured Lilith. "That guy who just walked in…he's looking for somebody. See how he's just standing there, blocking the door? He's looking around. Yep, he sees the traitor, making a beeline for her."

"Mm-hmm, I see."

The server arrived with their beer and pretzels. "Here ya go ladies, enjoy and let me know it you need anything else."

"Thank you, will do," responded Lilith. "Okay, let's watch and see what's up." Sarah nodded in agreement.

"Hey! I can hear them," said Sarah in a stage whisper.

"Shhh! Keep your voice down," muttered Lilith. "Edgar rocks, I didn't know he rigged our ear thingies so we could hear Miss Twat's conversation. Cool."

"I know, right?" Sarah said, barely audible this time. Lilith smiled at her friend and nodded. Both women pretended to be enjoying their Guinness and pretzels while listening to Melonie's conversation.

"You got my stuff, Mel?" asked the guy who had just walked in and searched for her.

"Yeah, I got it. You got the cash?"

"Yep, right here, one G. Five hundred for the, ah," lowering his voice, "for the pot and five hundred for the oxy."

"Alright, come on, follow me," said Melonie as she led her client to a booth that, lucky for Sarah and Lilith, was opposite where they were sitting. They could see and hear even better.

"Ok, slide the envelope across the table," directed Melonie.

The guy did as he was told. Melonie picked it up and looked in, then fanned the money she saw inside, counting that it was all there. Once certain the full amount was in the envelope, she reached into her oversized bag and pulled out a medium-sized paper sack, sliding it across the table to her client. He took it, opened…and, with a brief look inside, a big smile spread across his face. "Thanks Mel, see you next week."

Melonie checked her watch, then peered toward the door. Next, she pulled out her phone and stared at it for a while.

"Hey, Mel, you want a beer?" asked the bartender.

"Yeah, that'd be great, give me a Coors."

He grabbed a bottle and a frosted glass, and brought them over to Melonie. "How's it going with your plan? Is wonder boy all in?"

"Oh, yeah, he's more excited than I am about the whole thing. In fact, we're halfway there. The prima donna caught me earlier today with another client. Claimed she had evidence of it. Knew it was a lie when I went back to work. I checked in with my uncle and asked if he'd told her yet. He had, and he sent her ass home. I asked if he'd heard anything from her. Nope, not a word. Stupid-assed bitch! Todd's gonna have a great laugh when I tell 'im about it."

"Speaking of Todd, he's supposed to be in soon, isn't he?"

"Yep, we're gonna go over our story, make sure we're on the same page for court. Wanna make sure that preening princess goes away for a long time."

"You really think she'll get prison time for seducing Todd?"

"Oh, yeah, we've got some other surprises up our sleeves." Melonie looked at her phone. "Todd's got a friend who's crazy smart. He broke into her phone and laptop, just sitting outside her neighbor's house in a van with fake Spectrum signage on it. With the stuff he got, he made a bunch of deep fake videos showing the whore seducing many men and women in her office. I can't wait to see her face when she sees those show up in court. It's going to be outstanding," with this Melonie burst out laughing. "Oh yeah, she's going to prison. Yessir, that bitch is going down."

"Man, Mel, you don't have to remind me to stay off your bad side. Can I bring you anything else?"

"Yeah, bring me a nice big fat burger with some of those Cajun fries you got back there, and another Coors. I've got one more client coming and then Todd oughta be here."

"Your wish is my command. Oh, how's business since you switched…" — he looked around, making sure no one was listening, missing the two women just opposite who were, as they sipped harder on their pints of Guinness — "…from selling fentanyl to pot and oxy?"

Melonie shot him daggers. "You want the whole place to know? Geez, Manfred, keep it down. And yep, it's way more lucrative. Best decision I ever made. Now get me my burger and fries."

"On it," Manfred high-tailed it to the kitchen to get her order started, while the other bartender kept things running out front.

"My gawd, Sarah, didja hear that?" Sarah nodded, her eyes blazing. She gripped her pint tight and felt her facing burning with rage. "Take a breath, girl, and ease up on that glass before you break it. Remember, we don't want any attention." Sarah relaxed her grip, forcing herself to take a breath, exhaling as slowly as she could.

"Can I get you two another pint? And how about something to eat?" Their server was back.

"Uh, yeah, we'll take another pint and a couple of burgers with fries," said Lilith.

"Coming right up," and their server was off. Lilith, looking at Sarah, offered, "I think we'll be here a while; hope Edgar is doing ok out there." Sarah nodded.

"There he is, man of the hour! Come on over Todd, I've been waitin' for ya," said Melonie. "Perfect timing. I just finished my burger. You want anything?"

"Naw, I'm good. Wait 'til you see what've got," said Todd, looking happy as a pig in mud.

"Fabulous, let's get to it."

Sarah and Lilith exchanged glances. "Hang in there, keep it together, girl. I think we're about to grab the brass ring," Lilith said.

An hour later, Melonie and Todd headed out the door, arms wrapped around one another. All lovey-dovey. Sarah could have puked. "Those two make me sick."

"Yeah, me too. But, Sarah," Lilith said, so quietly Sarah almost didn't hear her. "We've got 'em."

"I hope so."

Lilith signaled their server over, "We'd like to settle up. Turns out my friend wasn't hungry. Can we take her burger and fries to go?"

"Of course. I have a Guinness or two, I can't eat either. It fills me up. I'll take that and wrap it up for you while you attend to the check. How's that sound?"

"Sounds fine to me. Thank you." Reading the server's name tag, she added, "Pat."

After they paid their check and Pat brought them Sarah's food, they waited another fifteen minutes before they decided it was safe to leave.

"You guys did great! As soon as I heard them talking about the deep fake videos, I hacked into Todd's laptop. Neither one of them is too bright. They used the bar's internet. It's not secured. What a surprise. Not," said Edgar jubilant as can be.

 "What do you think? Have we got them dead to rights?" Asked Sarah, wringing her hands together.

"I think so, but we need to run it by a lawyer first. Or, we could take it all to your boss, Sarah, have him get Melonie and Todd to drop the charges and then go after them in court. What do you think?"

Lilith spoke up before Sarah had a chance to say anything. "I think we should consult with a lawyer first."

"Yes, I'd feel more comfortable meeting with an attorney first," said Sarah.

"Okay, that's what we'll do," said Edgar. "Hey, I'm starved. Can I have your burger and the fries, Sarah?"

"Of course, here you go," said Sarah as she handed her leftovers to Edgar.

"Oh, my God! I'm so glad we went with the lawyer," said Sarah.

"I know, right?" Lilith asked.

"Everybody, bring it in," Edgar said, "it's group hug time and then out to celebrate!"

Ms. Chauncey, Sarah's lawyer, Lilith, and Edgar embraced in a big group hug.

"Thank you, Felicity, for all you've done," said Sarah, giving her another hug.

"You're very welcome. The three of you did a phenomenal job gathering the evidence. Sarah, Todd and

Melonie are going away for a long, long time and you can go back to work."

"Oh, no. I'm quitting as of today," said Sarah.

"What?" asked Lilith, Edgar, and Felicity in unison. "You heard me; I'd rather be strung up by my toes than go back to work as a substance abuse counselor. Too damn stressful."

"What will you do?" asked Lilith.

"Not a clue," said Sarah. "For now, I just want to go celebrate."

"Now THAT sounds like a plan," said Lilith. "Let's go."

"Won't you join us?" asked Edgar, looking at Felicity.

"Yes, you must," said Sarah.

"Absolutely, we won't take no for an answer," said Lilith.

"I won't argue," Felicity responded. "Happy to oblige."

Before leaving the courtroom, the group looked over at Todd and Melonie. As the cuffs were being put on them, they looked daggers at Sarah.

"You bitch!" Melonie screamed. "This isn't over! We'll get you; you just wait and see. Nobody messes with Melonie Taylor."

"Tell her, Melonie," said Todd. Whereupon Melonie wheeled around as best as she could, seeing as she was in cuffs, being gripped by the court officer. "You shut up! You scum! You rat! You DO know what happens to rats in prison don't you, Todd?"

Hearing that, Todd crumpled and began to cry. So much for his tough guy act.

Beaming ear to ear, Sarah, Edgar, Lilith, and Felicity Chauncey left the courtroom, arms linked.

49

"Hey," Edgar said, "we're sitting in a restaurant called The Good Fortune. Felicity, doesn't your name mean good fortune?"

"It sure does. And not just my first name, my last name means good fortune, too."

"Well, I'll be damned, Sarah, you were destined to win," said Lilith. "Everyone let's raise our glass to Felicity Chauncey, double the fortune!"

After they took a good long drink of their champagne, Edgar had an epiphany.   "Hey, I have an idea, Sarah, come work for me at my agency. You'd be great! I'll train you in the office and on the P.I. stuff. Together, I think we'd make a great team. What do you think?"

"I can help with any disguises you may need," said Lilith.

"And I can help with legal issues that'll come up. Trust me, they will come up. Consider it part of the job description," Felicity added.

Sarah looked around the table. Such kind, open faces. Faces she knew she could trust to have her back. It was kind of fun doing the spy thing.

"Why not? I'm in!"

"Another toast is required, server Elizabeth! We'd like another bottle of champagne, on me," said Felicity, a broad smile lighting up her face.

As they raised their glasses high, "To Sarah!" said Lilith.

"To Edgar!" echoed Sarah.

"To Lilith!" said Edgar and Sarah.

Edgar, Lilith, and Sarah, lifting their glasses even higher, "To Felicity, may her good fortune live on in name and practice!"

Chanah Wizenberg

Don Vaughan has made his living with words for more than four decades. His work has appeared in an eclectic array of markets, including Writer's Digest, MAD Magazine, Encyclopedia Britannica, Military Officer Magazine and Sky & Telescope. Don is the founder of Triangle Association of Freelancers (tafnc.com).

A Man Walks into a Burger King

Steven Tyler was wailing about love in an elevator as John eased the blue Civic off the interstate, down the exit and into the Burger King parking lot. He sat behind the wheel for a moment as the song finished, the setting sun casting long shadows against the building's exterior. The parking lot was empty, save for three other vehicles.

John had been on the road for almost five hours, and he was hungry. He braced against the winter cold as he exited the vehicle and walked quickly into the restaurant. The warmth felt good and he stood at the entrance for a few seconds, letting it wash over him. Only two other people were eating, a man with close-cropped hair and a young girl who looked maybe 11 or 12. They ate silently. The man's back was to the door.

At the counter John ordered a Whopper combo meal with a diet Coke. He sat two tables behind the man and girl as he waited for his food. He called home and Tina answered, excited to hear his voice. "Hi, sweetheart!" John said, trying to keep his voice low. "I just stopped for dinner, and I should be home in a couple of hours. Can I talk to Mommy?" Tina squealed something about Peppa Pig that John couldn't quite understand and handed the phone to her mother.

"How are you doing?" Catherine asked.

"I'm okay," John said, exhausted. "I signed off with the realtor on Mom's house this morning, so everything's all set. I'm at Burger King for a quick dinner, then I'll be back on the road."

"How long do you think until you're home?"
John calculated the mileage in his head. "Probably between 9 and 9:30."

"I'll be waiting," Catherine said quietly. "Stay safe."

"I love you."

"I love you too."

John's meal was waiting at the counter as he put away the phone. Returning to his table, he casually observed the man and girl. Neither had spoken since he had walked in, they merely stared at their trays as they ate. The man wore a brown camo jacket, blue jeans and heavy work boots. The girl wore a long-sleeved pink shirt, pink sweater, yellow corduroy pants and red sneakers. Her black hair hung loosely over her shoulders.

As he ate, John's thoughts turned to his mother, dead now nearly two months from the devastating effects of early onset dementia. She had just turned 68 when she died, in the nursing home, her mind long gone. One day she had known her son, her granddaughter, her many friends…and then she didn't. When the end came, she couldn't speak, couldn't eat, couldn't acknowledge in any meaningful way the middle-aged man who had been at her bedside for three terrible days waiting for the inevitable. John had held his tears until that moment, but couldn't refrain any longer. A nurse's aide hugged him as he sobbed at his mother's passing.

After her burial came the multitude of things that demanded John's attention. So many people and organizations and agencies to notify. So many of his mother's friends to console. He left her house for last, slowly going through her possessions, setting aside certain things he wanted to keep, then hiring a trash collection company to haul away the well-worn furniture and accumulated junk. He had wept again, just for a moment, as he locked the front door for the last time.

John was deep in thought when the girl accidentally dropped a packet of catsup on the floor. He glanced up as she bent down to retrieve it – and looked directly at him. "Please help me!" she mouthed, a look of panic on her face. "Please!" Then she sat back up and continued to eat, expressionless, one French fry at a time. The man glanced at her, then back at his phone.

John's heart raced. What the hell? He looked at the girl, expecting more, but she ignored him. Was this a trick? Were they messing with him? No. The panicked expression on the girl's face was genuine.

John took a pen from his shirt pocket, turned over the paper placemat on his tray and started to write the word "trafficked," then stopped. Would she know what that word meant? Hell, could she even speak English? John crossed out the word and under it wrote "Kidnapped?" in big letters. He held it up and waited for the girl's response. She raised her eyes, saw the message and nodded almost imperceptibly. John studied the girl's companion. He appeared to be in his late 20s, maybe early 30s. Though he was wearing a coat, John could tell that the man was well-built and strong. Certainly stronger than him.

John decided not to challenge the man. What if he was carrying a weapon? John didn't want to get shot, or unintentionally put the girl in harm's way. After a moment, he went to the men's room, telling the young woman at the counter, "I'm not quite done yet." She nodded.

The 911 dispatcher answered on the second ring. John spoke hurriedly, his voice hushed. He explained the situation with the man and the girl, how she had dropped the catsup packet and how he had used a sign to confirm that she was being trafficked. "Can you please send an officer right away?" he asked.

"Not immediately," the dispatcher said. "There's a multi-car accident with fatalities three miles north of your location on I-95, and all available highway patrol and municipal police are on the scene. I'll send someone as soon as I can, but I can't tell you exactly when that might be."

"What should I do?" John asked.

"Don't confront the trafficker," the operator said. "Don't do anything to endanger yourself or the girl. If they leave, try to get the license plate number of their car and we'll follow up."

"Okay," John said.

Just leave. This isn't your problem. You have enough to deal with.

John instantly hated himself for the thought. He knew it was a lie. What if Tina…

After taking a calming breath, John exited the men's room and walked to the counter. "I'm still a little hungry," he said. "Could I please get an apple pie?" He took the food back to his table and ate slowly, observing the girl while pretending to check his phone. She didn't look up. Despair colored her face. John thought he saw a bruise on her neck.

"We're leaving," the man said suddenly. He wiped his hands on a napkin and dropped it on his tray.

The girl said something in Spanish, so quietly John barely heard her.

"Make it quick," the man said. The girl eased out of her chair and walked to the restroom.

John's mind raced. He looked behind him, out the window into the parking lot, now illuminated by bright halogen lights. No cops.

The man stood up as the girl returned from the restroom. She walked with a defeated shuffle, eyes on the ground.

As the man turned, John stood up, positioning himself between the man and the door. His heart pounded. "I know what's happening here," he said. "You're not taking the girl." He tried to sound strong, but his words tumbled out shaky and scared. The young woman who had taken his order looked up, concerned. Two other women joined her. The man was confused. "What?"

"You're not taking the girl," John said again. "I've called the police and they're on their way. Leave the girl. Just get in your car and go."

The girl's eyes grew wide as the man gripped her hard by the forearm. "I don't know what you're talking about, asshole," the man said. "She's my sister. Now get out of the way."

"Is that true?" John asked. The girl stared at him, unspeaking, terrified. She shook her head.

"Get out of the way," the man said again. "Don't make me hurt you."

"The police are on their way," John repeated. "Get in your car and drive away." He thought of the only other fight he'd ever been in, in middle school. He had lost badly, a humiliating defeat.

"What's the problem here?" asked the oldest of the women behind the counter, obviously the manager.

"This man is trafficking this girl," John said, not taking his eyes off his anticipated attacker. "I've called the police and they're on their way."

The man grew angrier. "I told you, she's my sister!"

"She's not," John replied. He braced himself for the man's inevitable charge. The man would try to punch him, he knew. Would try to take him to the ground and hurt him as badly as he could.

He was ready.

The man's eyes grew dark. "I'm telling you for the last time – get out of the way."

John didn't move. He stared at the man, challenging him with his silence. At that moment the girl broke free from the man's grasp and ran to the counter. The manager reached over, scooped her up and handed her to one of the other women. "Take her to the office and lock the door," the manager instructed. "Call the police."

The man stared at John, breathing hard. John stepped aside. "Go," he said. "Get the fuck out of here."

The man glanced at the women behind the counter, then back at John. The women were recording the moment on their phones. "I should kill you," the man growled. John said nothing. With a grunt, the man ran out the door and disappeared into the parking lot. Screeching tires announced his departure.

John collapsed into a chair, breathing hard. He realized he had forgotten to get the car's license plate number, but that's okay, he thought. The girl was safe. He noticed he was drenched in sweat as the manager brought him a cup of iced tea. "I have a daughter," she said softly.

"Thank you for what you did."

Two minutes later, a highway patrol car approached from the interstate.

John related his story while the trooper took notes. As they talked, the manager brought the girl out from the back office. She held the girl's hand protectively. The girl looked at the trooper, then at John. John smiled at her and she smiled back. Then, almost as an afterthought, she ran across the restaurant and heaved herself into John's arms.

They held each other tightly for a long minute, neither speaking. The girl was dirty and smelled sour, as if she hadn't bathed in days. The bruise on her neck was more evident now, the shape of strong fingers. John forced himself not to think about what she had endured.

"What's your name, sweetheart?"

"Alexis," the girl replied. Her face suddenly scrunched and she began sobbing, wetting John's coat with her tears. The manager gave her a chocolate ice cream cone and she and John sat quietly, side by side, until another trooper arrived, a woman with a broad face and a ready smile. She talked briefly to the first trooper, then gently approached Alexis.

"I'm Trooper Alvarez, and I'm here to keep you safe and help you get back to your family," she said. "Hablas español?"

Alexis nodded. "Si."
Trooper Alvarez began talking to Alexis in Spanish. John listened, but understood little, assuming particular questions based on Alexis's answers. Every few minutes he gave her hand a gentle, reassuring squeeze.

When she was done, Trooper Alvarez turned to John. Her first words startled him. "You probably saved this girl's life," she said. "From what she's told me, she was being groomed for a horrific existence."

"So what happens now?" John asked.

"We'll take Alexis to the hospital so she can be examined for…" She paused. "So the doctors can make sure she's all right. At the same time, we'll work to find her family. She's from North Carolina, so it shouldn't be difficult."

"That's good," John said. He took a business card from his wallet. "Please let me know if there's anything my wife and I can do to help."

Trooper Alvarez said something to Alexis in Spanish and the little girl stood up to leave. John looked down at her with a grin. "You were very brave today," he said.

Alexis squeezed his hand tightly. "Thank you," she said in halting, accented English. "Thank you for helping me."

After the troopers had departed, John called Catherine. Tina answered again. "Hi, Daddy!" she squealed.

"Mommy's letting me stay up so I can see you when you get home!" Everything was a declarative statement with a four-year-old.

"I can't wait to see you, sweetheart," John said. "I miss you so much. Can I talk to Mommy please?" Catherine came to the phone. "Everything okay?"

"Yes, but I'm going to be a lot later than I thought," John said. He related the story of his confrontation with the trafficker.

"For God's sake, John, you could have been shot," Catherine said, shocked and angry. "What were you thinking?"

"I know," John replied. "But I had to do something, Cat. I couldn't…" He stopped talking as the magnitude of what had just occurred overwhelmed him.

"I'm glad you're okay," Catherine said, calmer now. "I love you, sweetie. We'll talk more when you get home. Please be careful on the road."

John started to hang up, then paused. "Let me talk to Tina again," he said.

"Sure." Catherine handed the cell phone to the toddler at her feet.

"Hi, Daddy!" Tina shouted. "I made cookies with Mommy tonight!"

"I'm sure they're delicious," John said, reveling in his daughter's little-girl sing-song voice. "I just wanted to tell you how much I love you, Baby Doll."

"I love you, too, Daddy! Come home quick, 'kay?"

John said goodbye to the women in the restaurant and walked slowly to the Civic, his coat pulled tight. He still had another four hours on the road. On the radio, Freddie Mercury sang of Scaramouche.

Don Vaughan

Barbara Burns, Ph.D. is a published writer, educator, naturalist, and retired psychologist. She is a graduate of Rice University, a doctorate from U. Missouri, and a Master's from U. Tennessee. She is a past member of Southern Highland Craft Guild and a member of TAF. Her activities include researching, writing, painting, fossil hunting, and birding.

Colorado Blue

Walking near the road's crusty edge and poking her cane at a piece of chert, she said, "It's a wonder I can still do this, isn't it? Isn't it, Jake? But I always said, didn't I? I always said I'd keep moving, even if I had to crawl out and dig a parsnip for dinner." I'm about that far gone she nodded to herself--but not yet, not quite. Ideas tumbled in her head like tiles in a bingo basket, except they sometimes stuck together in clumps and thumped around like tennis shoes in a dryer, until she forced the spinning to stop. Glad to be out again on the high desert road, she put her cane down by a pale, bristly bush and stood straighter.

Stretching out twiggy arms as far as she could, she lie her head back and marveled at the extent of sky— enormous-- an all-knowing blue, shielding the world. It was the same blue as the lid of her compote bowl, a blue that kept everything safe from disorder and disruption. Bending again, to release Jake's collar, she gave him permission to run loose. He sped off through the brush, blond tail flying high, zigging and zagging, thinking he was still chasing antelope.

Her right arm covering her eyes, she scanned the broad scrubland, her land, stretching limitlessly in every direction, unfurling from her slight frame until it bumped into Mount

Blanca still laced with mealy snow. With every puff of wind, her thin tee-shirt outlined her ribs and plastered her hair against her skull in frail, gray strands. She examined the sand. It was all of a color unless you looked closely at the grains, white, tan, yellow, and black. The black particles sifted to the top if you shook a pinch in your palm. It was just ground-up mountain, she knew, but couldn't help wondering how such an elegant, structured thing could end up as a pile of mineral grist. Everything changes, even though they're the same—a puzzle.

The range of low growth that covered the valley floor changed little with the seasons. Like the sand, the colors were muted-- dust-dredged and green edged with tan, ochre, and umber.

 Woolly vegetation lay over the San Luis valley floor like an old green army blanket—one a huge beast might have crawled from under and left rumpled, with unkempt pleats. After she bent to retrieve her cane, and as her spine returned to its old lady curve, she saw something scuttle away without dislodging a single grain of sand. A horned toad. It disappeared-- gray, light gray, dark gray, almost gray, into a salt bush. She liked it here, where all was subdued, no egregious colors blaring. Even the markings on desert wildlife were restrained—soft browns, tans, creams, and grays. Her attention to desert life was acute. Creosote bush, sage sparrows, kangaroo rats, darkling beetles, each awakened in her a profound connectedness to the private lives of the shy creatures that roamed over this high-valley floor.

 Her observations, always keen and constant, permitted identification of the faintest paw print, hoof, or cricket nick in the sand. The delicate patterns suited her need for subtlety and nuance. She'd never liked discordance or raucous sounds, never cared for Bartok, remembering only the odd fact that he was born in the Polish town of Nagyszentmiklos.

She turned, tiring, and began making her way back to the small trailer, resting isolated, pale and sheltered, in a slight hollow. On the back deck, which she had cobbled together herself, remembering her aunt's motto, "If it needs doing, do it," she lowered herself to a wind-battered rocker, and thought about the blue-lidded compote while she waited for Jake. Originally, she hadn't appreciated 'The West," coming as she did, from the mountains of Appalachia, where charm and leafy extravagance couldn't be matched—and where everything was green.

But her judgment matured in time, as she absorbed the sheer power of the desert, taking into her heart all its unfathomable force, the over-the-top grandeur, and its incalculable expanse, where every breath she took blended with ether-threads of the Indian souls still diffusing through the desert air. Her partner had brought her to this place, and had given her the blue compote bowl, saying that it held the Colorado sky. Now it held only ashes and the remains of their life—the one thing she thought would never change.

As she rocked, and looked across the open land at Mt. Blanca, she saw Jake bounding toward her. The sight nudged her out of the mental loop she'd entered, and she stopped the tumbling tiles long enough to welcome him.

Before another week had passed, she and Jake were on the sandy road again, looking for artifacts. A few days prior she had uncovered a dimpled stone, stained with red ochre--a paint pot. Today, when she poked at a promising basalt chip, she heard Jake's 'alert' growl, and looking up, she saw a large, brilliant, royal blue pick-up parked on the road across from her trailer.

Shining silver, its eight-lug, hubcaps sparkling in the sun,
while nearby, a tall man was doing something in the road. As
soon as his truck raced off, leaving a roiling trail of music
and sand, she hurried down the road to see what he'd been
up to, and found a sign staked in the ground:

Coming Soon

WILD-ACRES TOWNHOUSES LOT 62

Lament

When you're old,
you can't stop dying.

Where are the days
that were so real?
Where are the lawnmowers with no motor?
Where is my grandmother?

Where's the ache I used to feel
at your face in the wind--
hair brow-blown,
faded now, and worn.

My hand, brown spots and blue
holding yours, holding you
and know we're both
lost in the quarry.

Can't get out,
can't climb or shout.
earthquakes won't free us
until dirt has filled our heads
and those who look, see nothing.

What would you see, anyway,
looking in my brain
through the X-ray machines,
that used to be in shoe stores?

Bed Springs

(the day we were let out of school to
find scrap metal for the WWII war effort)

It was fall 1944 when I won
the war.
It was inexplicable.
It was victory. It was mastery. It was
my gift to
the world.
It was where
the war was won-- by me.
released from school,
restraints lifted,
we ran the fields, arms spinning, looking—
in backyards, in
trash bins, alleys, and cull
de sacs, in
garbage dumps, drainage
ditches,
in weeds and
stickers,
empty barns, we looked--
in chicken
houses—everywhere.
looking,
scrap metal for the war!
scrap metal for the war!
pulling our wagons, and
finding--
iron pipes, tin cans, crank shafts, silver,
shoes, pots,
wires, tubes, wheels, fenders, spools

clothes-line
poles, tools, and rusted
screws, fan blades,
hammer ends.
Who would find the most?
Who would win the war?

And then I found them!
Bed Springs!
lying in the field,
crusted and waiting
for me!
Bigger than anything!
Bigger than a hotel!
Huge, they wouldn't fit,
no matter how, they would
not fit my wagon,
but, I
managed. I
laid them down, found a way to
take them in.
dragged them in, and
pulled them down the
rutted lane,
and turned them in
at the end of the game.
I won.
I did my part.
I saved the world - - - -

And it was the only thing I ever did
that mattered.

Murder at the Market

It was already 20 minutes past time! The smell of the cantaloupes was making me sick. I wish I'd chosen a different place to wait-- -the watermelons, maybe, or by the collard greens. Too late, she'll be coming any minute--can't chance it--missing her. The market's aisles between tables of fruits and vegetables were absolutely jammed, jammed, with hordes! My back was beginning to hurt. Veggies piled on every surface and rolling off across the floor, apples, too. A mess. And the stench, rotting fruit, pound cake—the bakery was just behind. The place was mobbed, every kind of person in the world! Old butt-less men with falling-off pants. Mothers in too-short shorts and no bras, pushing strollers. Sparrows under the eaves, shitting everywhere. What the Hell! End of July and tomatoes on every stand.

She'd be right back, she said-- uh huh, like I ever believed that! Yo! There she is! In that silly yellow T-shirt—with the wrinkled sleeves, it'd been in a wad in the dryer ever since, ever since she can't fold worth shit! I stood there, waiting, to see if she saw me or even looked for me. I watched a gay couple walk past-- you could sure tell who was who with that couple, the 'husband' had a watermelon on one shoulder—Biiiiig Man!

A gorgeous kid with auburn curls rolled by in a stroller with a mother. They stopped to look at the heirloom tomatoes, but when the mother saw me staring, she turned the stroller sideways so I couldn't see. Automatic, like locking the car door when a homeless man walks by. She maybe sensed something. Can't be too careful.

My wife finally looked in my direction.

"Hey," I called, she turned, and seemed to move faster. I watched a moment to get it right, raised my arm, checked the silencer, get it? Silence her—and I did! She moved closer for a minute, but I could see she had paled. She wobbled a little to one side and then fell forward just in front of an old man with a cane who also fell, followed by shouts and whoops and hollers, you'd think they'd never seen a person on the ground! People backing away and people bending over.

My wife was not moving. Why is it when you're dead, you get so incredibly flat? All juices and ethers get sucked right out. Always a surprise how expressed they get. The body just expels life, leaving skin on skin lying there like a quilt without a filling. I slowly turned, while several people, including a full-of-himself black kid, were calling 911. I walked along the edge of the emptying aisle in the center of the market, away from the noise, until I was far enough away that no one was reacting to anything beyond the price of peaches. When I stepped out into the parking area, rain sprinkles were falling, and had already caused a mass of clogged cars. Sprinkles! God help us, people are so unutterably stupid!

The next morning, I watched the scene on the news. I was already packed. I showered, brushed my teeth, and pooped. I left the motel security card neatly on the bed, and walked to my car. I knew I wouldn't get there until late evening, but that was OK, I had lunch packed and could eat a bite if I got hungry. I like my own food, it's clean.

The road ahead was mine, the evening would be mine, too. Highway 40 over the Smoky Mountains is a lovely drive, especially if you're traveling east. You do have to keep your eye on the road, though, lots of curves and lots of 18 wheelers weaving in and out, acting like fucking kings of the road. Emergency downhill break ramps around every corner in case

one of them gets uppity or brakes fail. I was never lucky
enough to catch that happening. The sourwoods were
blooming, my favorite Tennessee tree. It was after ten
o'clock when I pulled in the driveway.

As I expected, the lights were on. Nancy was awake
and waiting for me. Nancy was the neat one, always clean
and ironed! I wanted her to be ready for me. She always
knew what I wanted, knew my mind. Sometimes I didn't
even have to tell her. What she didn't know was that I was
tired, tired of her working so hard-- to please me. Actually, I
was sick of it! What kind of spunk is that? She heard my car
door shut and came to the door-- backlit. I walked around to
the passenger side. I could see she had something in her
hand. Maybe it was my drink! She knew I'd want a drink,
silly thing! I pulled the gun from the passenger seat, raised
my arm and sighted down the barrel---- there was a funny
noise, and before I could pull the trigger, everything went
black, I was falling, I could feel blood burbling---maybe I
just need to rest a minute.

Barbara Burns

69

K Ann Pennington is a social studies teacher who has traveled over 30,000 miles around the United States by RV. Pastimes include examining primary source materials and performing field research, especially on the Civil War. She is working on an historical novel that takes place on the Rocky Mountain frontier just after the Civil War.

Down in Pisagitoches

My new husband had warned me about his mother. On the way to her house for the first time, my honeymoon excitement gave way to an anxiety pit in my stomach. We drove on long engineered causeways over the swamps of his childhood. He assured me his mother had sent well-wishes, that she felt happy for us.

Opting not to wear a current fashion blouse and miniskirt to meet her, I donned a sensible tweed pantsuit and kept the ensemble light on jewelry—only a watch and my wedding band. I might not have been out for a night of dancing, but I still had to be me, and in this case, I'd chosen to present my professional side. She'd know the truth about what I was sooner or later. Might as well make it sooner.

I studied the name of my husband's hometown on a gas station map.

"Say it once more: Pisagitoches. Pa-sag-a-tuhsh," Webb said.

Under pressure to perform, I spit out,"Pigsackachess."

He laughed. "Get used to some of the Indian names down here. I used to attend church over in Cooxiehouma."

70

"Do Wah Diddy Diddy" by Manford Mann blared from the car radio and Webb shouted, "Better enjoy this 'Top of the Pops' now. Once we're at Mama's, she'll allow none of the Devil's work. I used to listen to Memphis a.m. radio under the sheets in the middle of the night so she couldn't hear it. Hell, Uncle Donny bought me the radio. He gave it to me, wrapped in newspaper, when we'd gone fishing at Papaw's catfish pond. I never showed it to Mama, and she's never once brought it up. I see now that Uncle Donny meant for it to be our secret. Oh, and I read the newspaper, too."

My heart warmed on top of the heavy awe it held. I'd married a man who'd not been allowed a radio as a child, and I felt sorry for that little boy being so deprived. But the United States Army changed his direction and put him on the path of his career as a radio announcer.

I clutched my Enid Collins Sagittarius bucket tote bag. Mom had given it to me to match my honeymoon outfits. It contained my Congress of Racial Equality lapel pin, my paper wallet I picked up while working as a Red Cross "Clubmobile Girl" in Korea, and our wedding pictures. I worried about those more than anything. Was that naive? Sure it was. This entire endeavor of ours was. The pictures might arouse a difficult beginning without an easy end clouding my beloved union forever. I'd been at the DMZ in Korea and marched in some rough civil rights events, but meeting my new mother-in-law for the first time intimidated me more than anything.

My freshly wedded drove our silver 1964 Chevy II. We'd purchased the car off the showroom floor for each other as a present in honor of our nuptials. Webb never had a new car before; neither had anyone in his family.

He meant to impress his mother. And smooth things
over. He smiled at me like he felt the weight, too.
We approached the yellow-trimmed, white aluminum-sided
trailer at the end of a narrow unpaved road beneath an
extended canopy of pines. A collar-less hound followed the
car, but Webb told me not to worry. His mother kept Buster
for protection even though the dog would harm no one,
unless kisses brought death.

The skinny trailer door opened before we exited the
Chevy, and there she stood in her cotton shift dotted with
yellow daisies. She held a lit cigarette between two of her
tan fingers; her other hand clutched an extra-tall glass of
iced-tea.

"Took y'all long enough to get here." She hardened
her brow.

I smiled but also rested my face to look natural, not
too smiley. I gripped Webb's hand.
He grinned and said, "Mama, I told you we were stoppin' to
get ya these," then revealed the bouquet of red roses he'd
been holding behind his back. "They're like you like, from
the A&P."

She scowled, then dragged off the cig and checked
me out, up and down.

"Get in the house, Buster. If ya ain't pissed yet,
y'aint gonna."

The dog ran in, with its tail down tight against its
rear.

"Why you ain't in uniform, Webb. I like seein' you
like that."

"Awe, Mama, we just come off our honeymoon in
Memphis, and I'm ready to play civilian. Hey, this here's
Lisa."

I stepped forward. "Pleased to meet you Ms. Tate."
"Ms? Honey, I'm a Mrs."

72

"Mama, please—"

"You all gettin' fancy on me? Cain't keep up with you. They teach you that up in Washington D.C., Lisa? Gettin' fancy and changin' who women are?"

"No, ma'am." Webb made sure I knew to address her that way. "Just a different style of speaking, ma'am. Thank you." I averted my gaze at first, but then resolved to stand strong and look her in the eyes. I'd done nothing to be ashamed of.

"Huh." She stared, maybe glared. "Y'all ate yet? Y'anta come in for some cornbread and buttermilk? I got some fried okra and coconut cake, too. Just watch how much you pass by your lips, Lisa. You don't want it for years on your hips."

"The food sounds wonderful after traveling, ma'am." That might have sounded like complaining over coming to see her. "You're Webb's favorite cook," I said, trying to be as sweet as the cake. Webb agreed and praised his mother. I was on the right track.

Inside the mobile home, two quick cigarette puffs in a row filled the kitchen with swirls of gray haze. The fog hung over us throughout the meal.

Webb kept the conversation going while we dined on a simple supper of scratch-made cornbread and chicken dressing accompanied by fresh produce—sliced tomatoes and onions, pickled jalapenos, and simmered green beans—grown by Mrs. Tate. She asked about my parents and repeated some of the things Webb had told her about them, like how my dad was a sheep rancher in the Rockies and my mom died when I was young. The last part seemed to touch her. She stopped asking questions and smoked while we finished supper, actually taking drags at the same time as food filled one side of her mouth and she chewed.

73

Afterward, we sat together in the front room with what had to be dozens of cactus plants along the windowsill. Mrs. Tate smoked and drank iced tea with her legs curled under her as she sat on the sofa.

"You ever watch game shows, Lisa? Let's Make A Deal and Concentration? She picked her teeth with a toothpick she'd selected from a collection of toothpicks in a little glass finger bowl, then she returned the chosen one back to the group. "I like Concentration the most. I've watched it—I don't know for how long, do you, Webb?"

He tried to calculate the years and I spotted a five gallon bucket over by the deep freezer that stood under the giant portrait of Jesus radiating light. Webb must have noticed because he said, "That bucket is full of Mama's sauerkraut. Mama, tell Lisa how you make your delicious kraut."

Between drags Mrs. Tate described cutting the cabbage just the right size and how she used a plate to hold it down when it wasn't being smashed periodically with the end of a broom handle.
She never sounded happy, or sad, or mad, or excited. And always in the background, a televangelist preached on TV. Mrs. Tate kept the volume up, but I tried to share our wedding photos with her, anyway.

"These are for you, ma'am," I said in a clear voice as I handed her the black and whites of her son's marriage ceremony at the Washington D.C. city hall with a maid of honor and best man as witnesses. "I had duplicates made."

"Isn't Lisa a lovely bride, Mama?"

Mrs. Tate snatched the pictures. "Y'all didn't want no family there?" She studied the images.

"What in the Lord—" Her finger traced my Maid of Honor's dark-skinned arm for a moment. "Webb, get me them scissors from the top drawer this instant."

Webb didn't move.

"You know where they are. You lived here long before that Army took you away from me."

"But Mama—"

"I'll get 'em myself, then." She crossed the room to the kitchen. A drawer slid and creaked.

Webb went in to see and came back with flushed cheeks, grinding his hands together. He pulled me over to a corner behind the metal stand of potted Christmas cactus plants.

"She's cutting Althea and Vernon out of our wedding picture."

"But, Webb …"

He shoved his hands in his pockets. "I tried to warn you—"

"I know. Doesn't make it less shocking, though when you don't come from it." I intended to keep my voice down, but I didn't. He grabbed my hand.

"You're right." For him, I lowered to a raised whisper. "My history with Althea in the Red Cross, our participation in the march on Washington, that she'll be the godmother to our child when you and I have one—they're realities your mother will have to face."

Webb looked me in the eye. "That's right, Lisa." He hadn't let go of my hand.

Mrs. Tate and her frown returned. She dropped the adulterated picture on the coffee table.

Mr. Television Preacher spoke of America's hardening attitude as the nation and world cried out for help. Cutthroat ideological battles. Revolution. The need for love and Jesus.

Webb and I sat there with his mother, glancing at one another and around the room, unsure of what more to say.

Justice for Liberty: What Will We Do?

And the corpse whispered in her ear: "What will we do with
the body?"
It should've been chilling, her victim speaking to her like
that from the dead, oh, flat dead.
The blood had long since drained into pools that might've
been mistaken for spilled merlot.
Skin like marble, even some black veins; eyes shrunken in
dark sockets; eyes still somehow screamed for more oxygen.
But she kicked the torso—rubbery; dense like a tree trunk.
She slapped the empty (in life and death) head back and
forth a few times.
All the things she wished the central core of the panopticon
would've mandated, things We had to do.
But she alone did it.
The corpse began the rot steeped by a so-called second
coming of Jesus.
We all felt it
and the twisted wind that came in His name.
Yes, she was asked what she'd do with the body,
and she knew chopping it up into little pieces would not
stop the blood-fed soil,
for the crucifixion had happened again.
So, too, the new age martyr.
What would she do with the body?
She finally replied, "Who cares what happens to the body?
It's what you do with the soul in the after that matters
and then, only then, maybe, you can revive the dead."

K Ann Pennington

Rebecca Dalton has been reading science fiction since she was a kid and her mom introduced her to it. She writes stories that explore what our future could look like, and all the ways that people can make the world better by working together. Visit her at RebeccaDalton.net.

A Moment in Time

The day Charlotte discovered time travel she was so exhausted she should have been more worried about accidentally blowing things up than about making world-shattering, Nobel prize winning scientific discoveries. The possibility of blasting off half the lab, herself with it, was infinitely more probable than anything else.

The calculations for stabilizing her wormhole were incredibly sensitive, and in hindsight she had no business messing with them while sleep deprived. One misplaced subset out of twenty pages of calculations and she'd destabilize the entire thing and potentially release a quantum backlash so big it would destroy everything around it. Hence, the explosion.

If she hadn't been so hopped up on caffeine (her fourteenth cup today) and adrenaline (she'd gotten a second wind about three hours ago) she'd have appreciated the danger. Instead she'd gotten a flash of insight so clear she'd known exactly what to do and didn't even question it.

She'd texted Dan immediately that she wouldn't be home until very late.

He responded, "That exciting?"

"Even better. I'll explain later. Kiss Emmy for me when you put her down."

Charlotte spared a pang of regret that she wouldn't see her four-month-old daughter before she was put to bed for the night, but consoled herself with the reassurance that she'd take the first night waking after she got home and would give her all the cuddles she could want then. She didn't look forward to the interrupted sleep, but it was par for the course at this point. She hadn't gotten a full night of sleep since she'd been seven months pregnant. She'd frankly forgotten what that even felt like.

She'd finished keying the last of the calculations in and now her finger hung poised over the Enter key. Had she gotten everything right? Yes – she'd triple checked every last bit of it. Was she ready to change history? Absolutely.

She hit the key.

There was a flash of brilliant light in the space off to her right, the area she'd designated for this experiment. It was a seven foot by seven-foot square of floor space cordoned off by caution tape with a DO NOT ENTER – EVER! sign taped to it. Everyone who worked here knew to take such signs seriously, even the cleaning staff.

The light flared from a pinprick to the size of a basketball, then twisted and rotated, stretching into a flat circle that expanded out quickly until it hit the pre-determined size of six feet across.

Charlotte gaped. She'd believed she'd had the calculations right, had worked for three hours straight to get them all put into the program that controlled the wormhole's creation and stabilization because she was so sure it was right. And yet, she'd been wrong so many times before. How many days had she sat hunched over her laptop trying not to tear her hair out in frustration? All because she couldn't get the quantum strings to anchor where she needed them so she could open the wormhole where and when she wanted it.

She'd been tempering her optimism with a quiet certainty that this would fail like the other attempts, and now that it hadn't, she was astonished.

It was real.

She got up and walked over to the square and paused in front of it. She had a clear image of the grey concrete block wall behind the wormhole. She'd never have even known the space-time phenomenon was there except for the blinding white light creeping out from the perfectly round edge of the wormhole's mouth. And also, the digital clock with a date stamp attached to the wall behind it.

She'd started trying to prove this theory three years ago. She'd roped off the area, informed anyone who would listen that entering could be potentially fatal, and then hung up a clock with a readout big enough to be read from across the room so she could tell immediately if her time calculations had worked.

They'd worked. The date on the clock read two years prior, three o'clock in the afternoon.

Charlotte laughed. It had worked.

She ran over to her desk and grabbed the Marie Curie bobblehead doll her mom had given her on her tenth birthday, when she'd declared that she'd wanted to be a scientist. She walked towards the wormhole, then stopped. Best to pick something else. She couldn't stand for the doll to be destroyed. She put the doll back and grabbed her plastic coffee mug instead and tied a string to it.

She went back over to the wormhole, stepping over her caution tape barrier so she could stand in front of it.

"Here goes," she whispered, and chucked the mug through the circle. It hit the ground beyond the circle with a crack, then clattered across the floor until it hit the wall and rolled to a stop. She was relieved to see it still looked whole, and hadn't vaporized or something. She edged to the side so

79

she could peer around behind the wormhole, taking care to keep the string away from the edge (she didn't want it accidently sliced).

No mug. The date and time were correct for today, though it was about to be tomorrow in ten minutes. Weirdly, the back of the wormhole looked like a flat black circle. Not a matte finish, but a circle so black it seemed to suck all the light into it. She shivered. She'd known that the wormhole connected two black holes at either end of a tunnel and contorted them, so they pulled energy from one end of the wormhole to the other, but she hadn't considered the practical implications of that.

Was there an open black hole on the other side of her wormhole? She and everything in the room weren't being sucked into it so… possibly not? That was definitely a matter for testing.

Not tonight, though. Tonight she just needed to know that this thing was working. She stepped back in front of the wormhole and was happy to see her string was still whole. She gave it a tug and pulled the mug back up and into her hands.

It looked exactly the same as it had before she'd tossed it over: white plastic with MOMS RULE! written across the side in pink, and the ring of coffee from her last cup dried on the bottom when she peered inside.

"Oh, my god," she whispered.

Suddenly she could think of a dozen things she wanted to do, but she stuck to the plan she'd put together in case she'd actually succeeded. She called it the How Not to Disintegrate Yourself Protocol, but really it just meant making sure the wormhole wasn't dangerous to living things before using it. She considered getting more coffee, but then decided that if she drank any more tonight she was guaranteed not to sleep at all once her head hit the pillow, and she definitely couldn't afford that. She'd just have to power through.

Her office plant went first. It was a blooming purple orchid, and a perfect choice. Orchids were so sensitive you could kill them any number of ways. Too much or too little water, too much food, not enough humidity, too much sunlight, not enough sunlight… Charlotte figured if an orchid could make it through okay that was a good sign. Plus she'd stuck a sensor into the moss around it that would send readings back to her.

She set an alarm on her watch for one minute, put the pot on the edge of a long, flat board and slid it through the wormhole. She watched it carefully for signs of wilting, singeing, or anything else. Nothing happened. The alarm on her watch went off and she pulled it back and took it to her desk to check her laptop.

The sensor had sent readings, just like it was supposed to, only there was way more data than she was expecting. Instead of the one minute worth of readings there were 60 minutes. She sat staring at the screen, not comprehending, until the answer seemed to smack her upside the head.

"There's a time dilation with the crossover!" Was that something inherent in travel through wormholes, or were her calculations causing it? She scrubbed her hands over her face. No way to tell right now. She could dig into her calculations later on, when she was fresh. In the meantime, she could read through the data she did have.

There was a small spike of energy as the plant crossed the threshold back and forth, but nothing the human body couldn't deal with. No abnormal readings for temperature, energy, radiation, air quality, or pressure. It didn't look like anything would be crushed, fried, vaporized, or otherwise mangled while going through.

81

"Perfect," Charlotte whispered, and went to find her next test.

Pinky lived in the corner of her lab in a multi-room complex that covered the top of a waist-high bookshelf holding notes and resources. This late at night he was awake and running in his wheel. Charlotte took the lid off and reached in to gently lift the white mouse from his cage. She turned him over and attached sensors to his chest and the top of his head, then slipped him into a small travel box with a handle on the top.

He tried to climb the walls as she went to attach the lid, but she nudged him back and fastened it on. She carried it to her desk so she could initialize the sensor and make sure it was broadcasting correctly, and watched him through the clear plastic. He sniffed and climbed around the edges, and she smiled. She'd had him for longer than her daughter had been alive. She'd gotten him as a potential test subject when she'd started working on the theory, and he'd been her little companion ever since. He liked to sit on her shoulder and nibble crackers sometimes while she worked on her equations. She got a sudden lump in her throat at the idea of sending him through the wormhole and she had to blink back tears.

"You'll be just fine," she promised the mouse. She busied herself with checking the readings to stop thinking of all the ways it could go wrong to send a living thing through a wormhole. Nothing had blown up so far. "The orchid was fine, my sensors are fine, everything is fine."

She lifted the lid and dropped a few treats inside. "Good luck," she whispered. He scrambled to eat them while she carried him over to the wormhole. She attached his little cage to a long stick with a hook at the end.

"Here goes," she muttered, and slid the cage through.

Pinky let out a tiny squeak when he crossed the threshold and then circled around the cage a few times, then he went back to his snacks and enjoyed himself. It would have been a completely normal scene except for one thing: he appeared to be moving in fast forward. It was as if she was watching a video of him that had been sped up to its fastest speed. Pinky nibbled his snacks, sniffed the cage, tried to climb the walls, laid down and seemed to go to sleep, then got back up and did it all over again. All at super fast speed.

"That is so weird," she muttered.

Charlotte let him stay over for five minutes, then anxiously pulled him back. She set the cage down on the table and pulled him out, but he was fine. He nosed up at her, red eyes looking everywhere as he sniffed around for more treats.

Charlotte put him on her shoulder and gave him one while she looked at her data. There was five hours of it.

"There's no way I can thoroughly review all this tonight…" she muttered.

But she didn't really have to. By backing out and looking at it all at once she could see there were no abnormal readings. There was a spike when Pinky had gone over and back again, a quick jolt of heart rate, blood pressure, and brain activity, but otherwise nothing unsafe. His readings currently coming from the monitor were also completely normal.

"It's safe," Charlotte said, leaning back in her chair so she could digest the implications of that. Every test indicated the wormhole was safe for living things. "It's safe!" she declared, picking up Pinky and kissing him on the top of his furry head.

"Well, of course we have to test a lot more extensively, and I need to get another set of eyes on these calculations to double check them, and we have to have it peer reviewed, and…" She trailed off. Pinky was gazing back at her quietly. "This is going to change everything."

That was the understatement of the century. The applications for time travel were so broad that it would change life as they knew it. She was practically guaranteed a Nobel Prize with this, as long as it stood up to testing.

"Is it weird that I'm too exhausted to be overjoyed?" she asked Pinky seriously. The clock on her laptop told her it was three in the morning. Very Late had been an accurate prediction. She had to close everything down, drive home, and hope Emmy didn't wake up ten minutes after her head hit the pillow. She probably wasn't getting to bed for another couple of hours. Her exhaustion slammed into her. "Guess the coffee ran out," she muttered.

She slipped Pinky back into his cage on the bookshelf with lots of treats and food (she felt bad that he'd been over there for five hours without any food) and sat back down to put her fingers on the keyboard and start the shut-down sequence.

Then she paused.

Time ran sixty times faster over there. Five minutes over here had been five hours over there. Ten minutes would equal ten hours. Ten long, quiet, uninterrupted hours where no one knew where she was and no one could bother her for any reason. It sounded like absolute heaven.

How much sharper would she be tomorrow at work if she had an actual full night of sleep? How much more could she enjoy her time with her daughter if she wasn't constantly going around with a sleep hangover that left her muzzy-headed all the time?

She stole a quick glance at the wormhole, as if she would get in trouble for thinking what she was thinking. But she could. Her department's director would definitely have strong words for her if he found out she'd used brand-new technology without even properly testing it.

But she had tested it, and who would know? No one. The building was officially closed at this hour, and as far as she knew none of her colleagues were running the kind of experiments that required around the clock monitoring.

She got up to slide the deadbolt on her door, ensuring that no one could enter.

She found herself standing in front of the wormhole debating with herself about whether she should do it, but it wasn't even really a question. She stepped through.

A low-level pain zinged through her, enough to make her jump and gasp but nothing more. Just like she'd expected. She turned around to see the view of her lab, looking exactly as she'd left it: disorderly from a long week spent bent over her laptop and ignoring everything else in favor of calculating. Every surface was littered with something: microwave meal plates, her favorite lab sweater, magazines, books.

She peered around the edge of the circle to see a perfectly neat and orderly lab, also exactly as expected. She'd set her destination date to the week she and Dan had gone on vacation for two weeks to tour Europe, and she'd cleaned up before she left.

Her gaze snagged on the cot up against the far wall. She used it on late nights (like this one) when an experiment required occasional monitoring overnight. It sat waiting for her with a pillow and blanket folded up neatly. It called to her, sleep a bigger siren song than anything else in the world. Was it worth the risk to indulge it? She'd already taken the biggest risk by stepping through, and she was so tired she felt like she might just fall over if she stood here any longer. Sleep won out.

Charlotte sunk down onto the cot and pulled the blanket over herself and was out like a light in no time flat.

She woke slowly, gradually becoming aware of the room around herself. It was silent, so unlike her own house in the morning. The sounds of Emmy crying or laughing or babbling, and Dan bustling around getting breakfast together, filtered into even her deepest sleep. There was no noise now in her lab, nothing to jolt her out of the deep slumber she'd just enjoyed. Nothing but the memory of last night.

She sat bolt upright on the cot and checked her watch. She'd slept for eleven and a half hours. She got up and ran for the wormhole, noticing that the side facing the room was the same pitch black she'd noticed the night before. Then she turned back and tidied up her blanket and pillow before rushing around the circle and back through the wormhole.

Pain zapped her and then she was back in her own time, staring wide-eyed around her lab. She had really done it. She'd gone through and back safely, had slept her fill for the first time in ages, and she was ready to tackle the biggest achievement of her career.

She was going to make history. And if she snuck off and stole herself an extra night of sleep here or there, well, that would only make her a better scientist and mother, right?

Rebecca Dalton

P.J. Black is author of the Selene Darke Series. Book One: Almost Darke. Book Two is due out in 2022. He is a gamer and avid science fiction/fantasy fan; enjoys anime, erotica, humor, and martial arts movies. He combines those elements into character-driven stories that explore the human condition. This happens under the supervision of his four black cats.

Paper Tiger

Gretchen sat with her back against the trunk of a particularly friendly maple tree. In her lap lay a magical tome filled with writhing text.

"So dull. Why don't witches ever index their grimoires?" No sooner had she uttered this than a rune attempted to hide beneath one of her thumbs.

"You get back there!" She shooed it back to its proper place on the page.

Suddenly, there was a beatific child standing before her. Without uttering a sound, the blonde-haired, blue-eyed beauty pointed towards the children in a nearby clearing. Reaching beneath the hatband of her pointy hat, Gretchen produced a silver page marker and slipped it between the pages. Only after she snapped the grimoire's lock did she feel the ancient book give its equivalent of a sigh.

When she entered the clearing, her green eyes followed the direction of a dozen tiny fingers pointing up into the branches of a tall white birch. For several moments, she simply observed the creature who had gained the attention of the gaggle of children in her care. Looking down at her from its perch was a small orange tabby kitten who appeared to be stuck.

As she approached the tree, Gretchen could feel its apprehension at having such a creature sitting amongst its branches. Placing both hands on its trunk, she gently pressed her forehead against the white bark. Then, whispering the language of druids, she very politely asked the nervous Betula Papyrifera if she could be of assistance.

After a few seconds, there came a creaking sound as the branch with the kitty slowly bowed downward until tiny feline could hop safely down onto Gretchen's shoulder. Her forehead still pressed against its trunk, Gretchen whispered her thanks to the tree, then turning, found herself surrounded by children who wanted to get a closer look at their furry guest.

 "Children, we don't know what this poor thing has been through, so I'm going to step away for few minutes to examine him."

The sounds of disappointed children followed her as she returned to her previous reading spot. She placed the kitten on the ground in front of her and said, "You can quit acting. I know what you are."

The kitten rolled his eyes at her, stood up on his hind legs and said, "I'm sure you do, witch. What concern is it of yours?"

"As one of the witches who cares for them, I'm here to ask you to leave our children be."

Crossing his little paws against his furry chest, in a hurt tone, he said, "You know I'm as much a victim here as they are. Before the dark fae kidnapped me, I was a human child."

"I've heard the stories. They stole your childhood and left you with the hunger."

"Then you know, asking me is a waste of time. If I don't feed on children, I'll die of starvation. All the sweet cream in the world won't keep me alive; So don't even try to bribe me with it. And I'm much too quick for a human to catch."

"What would you say to a deal?"

The fae kitten cocked his head to the side. "What kind of deal?"

"Rather than draining away all the life from a single child on a full moon, you could take sips from several of them through the month to keep your hunger from building past your ability to control it."

He appeared to give the matter some thought. "I'm not sure I believe you. You would willingly let me drain the life from the children?"

"No! Of course not! Not all of it. Perhaps a quarter. They would recover quickly enough. Then, in a week, you could tap another child and so on. We would need no single child more than once every few months. I'd even waive The Agreement after tonight so you could feed on the same child or a family member more than once."

"No one ever waives The Agreement."

"Your job will be to report to us if you see anyone who seems out of place. You stay well-fed and we have a local

89

dark fae who we know won't murder our children in their beds. Do we have a deal?"

"I guess we have a deal. When can you arrange my first feeding?"

She pointed to a massive black castle atop a nearby mountain. "Tonight, I'll slip you into the room of the little blonde girl. Afterwards, the other children in the castle will never be bothered by fae again. Is that not The Fae Agreement?"

The tiny kitty let out a chuckle that, for so high-pitched and diminutive a laugh, sounded surprisingly sinister. "So, it's to be the daughter of some servant girl used to protect the children of a great lord? This is your way of ingratiating yourself with him? I knew witches were scheming, but you're ruthless!"

A few hours after sunset, the fae kitten found himself inside a covered basket Gretchen had carried into the castle. By candlelight, he saw the beautiful young blonde girl he'd seen before. She was asleep on a massive, ornate bed in a room filled with fine furniture. "I thought this was to be a servant girl, not a member of the Darke Family!" he hissed.

"If anything goes wrong, they'll hunt me down and murder me!"

"It's fine," Gretchen hissed. "She's an orphan they've taken in as a playmate for the twins."

Still unwilling to leave the basket, the fae kitten looked down upon the sleeping child and thought, "In another decade, she'll be a beautiful young woman. Perhaps then the lord means to bed her and make her his playmate." A vile thought crossed his mind. "Or perhaps he already has." Aloud he whispered, "Fine. I'll meet you back at the birch tree later."

"No. I'm staying here to keep you out of trouble!" Gretchen hissed.

"I never agreed to that! I can always flee and pick a child at random."

The young witch seemed to weigh her options. "I'll expect you at that tree in one hour." He simply nodded.

Standing on the pillow, he looked down at her. Perhaps six years old, she had an angelic smile. Her lips were naturally red and shaped like a perfect cupid's bow. Her long, sunshine-bright blonde locks splayed out across the pillow and framed her face like a heaven-sent halo. After a few moments, wisps of white mist flowed from her mouth and nose and up into the mouth of the fae kitten.

The old wives' tales about cats sucking the breath away from babies began when a stray parent interrupted a dark fae cat's feeding; Faithful house cats had been paying the price for the crimes of the dark fae ever since. Unwilling to take such an affront lying down, cats soon became fae killing machines.

The fae were inhumanly fast, but over millennia, cats learned how to quietly lay in wait for them. Ironically, young mothers, fearful their faithful cat might harm their infant, continued throwing out the single most effective fae protection in existence; the irony was not lost on the cats.

91

Cats hate irony.

He never once gave a thought to abiding by his agreement, but as he drained her, the act soon shifted from one of feeding to one of intoxication. "So full of life! Perhaps she was destined to be a great witch!" He felt her struggling, but finally, her heart stopped. "I wish there had been another way, but you had the misfortune of drawing the attention of a twisted dark mage like Lord D…ACK!"

Faster than his superhuman eyesight could follow, a small hand shot up. Tiny fingers wrapped around his throat.

Abhidruh sat up and scolded, "Don't lie about our Michael!"

Gretchen stepped into the room and uttered a word of power. A heavy iron shutter rolled over the window and every candle in the room lit. "Thank you, sweet Abhidruh."

Gasping, the fae kitten said, "But I heard her heart stop beating!"

"You planned to murder her no matter what I offered."

"No! I just got carried awa…"

"Silence!" Her tone carried with it the razor-sharp edge of a newly sharpened bread-knife that left no room for doubt she would not hear another of his lies. Since the only thing that came to his naturally devious mind at that moment was another lie, he wisely chose silence.

She leaned down, putting her face so close it blotted out the fae kitten's world. "I know all about your kind!" she laughed. "You thought I was trying to bed Lord Darke? I'm his sister, the Lady Darke!" Her statement left the terrified fae dangerously close to soiling himself. "You attempted to murder a member of the Darke Family."

"The penalty is death," finished Abhidruh. Upon seeing the murderous intent in the youngster's eyes as she stared down at him over a mouth suddenly filled with razor-sharp teeth, the little fae finally lost his battle with his bladder.

In a pleading tone intended to invoke pity, the little fae kitten said, "With all due respect, it feels like you set me up to fail."

Gretchen's tone grew colder still. "No. We set you up to succeed! Had you stuck to our bargain, you would have been able to feed on Abhidruh every month. We would have asked no more of you than we do any of the other creatures we've helped to resettle here. Simply report to us if you see someone who does not belong. Unfortunately, you lied like the rest."

He knew any moment Gretchen would give this creature a nod and she would bite his head off and drink his blood like a drunkard uncorking a bottle with his teeth. He attempted to stall. "Excuse me, your Ladyship. Did you say there were others before me?"

"Of course. Did you not wonder why you were the only dark fae for hundreds of miles in any direction? Or why the light fae left you unmolested? This trap was created by one of my ancestors centuries ago. We use it whenever a dark fae wanders into our territory to give our children magical immunity. Every child in the county sleeps at the castle tonight."

He finally saw it. Within Darke County, The Fae Agreement now magically prevented him from even setting foot in a home with a child in it.

"I'd hoped you would realize how beneficial our arrangement could be for both of us, but…" She turned to go.

The once beautiful little demoness stared at the fae kitten through big wet eyes. She brought him close to her mouth and, with a mischievous grin, loudly clacked her monstrous teeth inches from his small furry face. He lost control of his bladder again. Despite her terrifying appearance, when she laughed at him, Abhidruh sounded like an angel giggling. Gretchen was closing the door when the terrified fae kitten gathered up every ounce of courage he had left and shouted,

"I have information!"

Without turning, the young witch paused just outside the doorway. "Speak."

Abhidruh grabbed him by his tail, and tipping her head back, dangled him over her mouth. As he watched, her jaw seemed to unhinge itself, allowing her to open her mouth wide enough to insert half a dozen kittens without one ever touching any of serrated, triangular teeth lining the sides. As he stared at the gaping maw of death below him, something broke. He shrieked to Gretchen's back, "They're preparing for war out west! Gods! Please don't eat me!" The little demon's pale hand slowly lowered him until he was inside

94

her pink mouth. Accepting his fate, he closed his eyes and waited for the end to come. He could feel the moist air surrounding him. He didn't know what to expect, but was surprised when he smelled… "Cinnamon?"

It felt like he'd dangled there for ages while he waited to be dropped down that pink gullet or snapped in two. Finally, he heard Gretchen's voice. "Abhidruh! Stop! I want to hear the rest."

The terrified fae kitten heard a sigh from his tormentor as she slowly lifted him out of her mouth. "Awww. I wanted to swallow him whole a few times so I could feel him wriggling in my stomach!" As she gently set him down without letting go of his tail, he opened his eyes. Her mouth had transformed back to that of a small child, albeit one with shark teeth. Looking down at him longingly, she asked,

"Please, Gretchen? Can I at least swallow him and throw him back up? I promise I won't chew!" Her promise would have been more convincing if her monstrous teeth didn't make obscene clacking sounds with each syllable.

Gretchen sat down on the bed and patted the Abhidruh on the head. "Let us see what he has to say. You may still get your snack." Then, looking at the trembling fae kitten, she said, "But first, I will have your name and information. Now."

He told her his name was Flax Thornbush and related his travels outside their western border. How he'd found a city without witches and began feeding regularly. As the bodies piled up, the authorities didn't care about the dozens of dead children. But even as he fed, he grew sicker and sicker.

The little demon child looked longingly at the fae kitten as he related his story of finding huge furnaces that ran day and night. "They're churning out swords and armor on a scale you can't imagine."

She closed her eyes and rubbed the bridge of her nose. "He's too afraid to lie and I can well imagine who those weapons will be used against." Lost in thought, her concentration was finally broken by the sounds of muffled screams. Snapping her eyes open, she saw Abhidruh smiling at her with a closed-mouth grin. The reason for the grin quickly became apparent, for between her red lips was Flax's fluffy tail frantically whipping back and forth.
"
Abhidruh!"

Abhidruh opened her mouth and placed the shaking Flax on the bed with uncharacteristic gentleness. "I was just playing. See?" She smiled. "Just my little girl teeth!" Gretchen took a deep breath. It was true, Abhidruh had shape-shifted again and had her human baby teeth back.

"Mistress! PLEASE! I did as you asked! Please don't let this one eat me!"

Gretchen looked down at the little orange tabby. Its fur was matted down with Abhidruh's saliva. She glanced over and saw the little demoness staring hungrily at the creature.

"I'm sorry, Abhidruh, but I can't let you eat this one."

Abhidruh began crying the inky black tears of an unhappy little demon girl. "That's the face of a tired five-year-old," thought Gretchen as she retrieved a handkerchief from within her skirts.

The little demoness cried so hard she began hiccupping. Her black tears popped and sizzled, leaving dark streaks - like sooty water on her white skin. Like a doting mother, the young witch pulled her close and soothed her as she wiped them away. "There, there, sweet girl. I know you had your heart set on eating this little fae, but he's done the Family a great service and we never hurt people who help the Family, do we?"

Even as she tried to stop crying, she was still gasping and hiccupping too hard to answer. Under the soothing ministrations of Lady Darke, she eventually calmed down enough to answer through her hiccups, "N… No."

Finally, the witch gently placed the handkerchief against the demon child's nose. "Blow." Afterwards, Gretchen pulled the cloth away and, with a flick of her wrist, it disappeared in a puff of smoke.

"Am I free to go?"

"Almost." From the bag, she produced a large dark red cookie and a small pink collar with a bell. "This is for being such a good girl."

"Yay! A blood cookie with sprinkles!"

Flax resisted the impulse to ask from what or possibly from whom the blood came. Instead, he sat patiently while the witch fastened the collar around his neck. After finishing, she flicked the tiny bell and uttered a spell.

"You work for the Darke Family now, so I will allow you to feed on Abhidruh once a month; But you'll wear a collar that makes it easy for us to find and catch you. I wouldn't try to remove it."

With a wave of Gretchen's hand, the iron shutter retracted.

"You're free to go Flax."

He had many questions, but the open window was more than his tiny fae heart could bear. With three supernatural bounds was up in the branches of a nearby tree.
Fae are a very curious lot and Flax more so than most. So it should be no surprise to know that he lingered to listen to the exchange between the young witch and her demonic ward.

"I'm sorry I played so rough, but he smelled so good."

"I know, sweet Abhidruh, but you did the right thing in the end."

Through a mouthful of cookie, she asked, "Can I sleep in your bed tonight?"

"Of course."

"Thank you."

"And Abhidruh, guess what?"

With the enthusiasm of a small child, she asked, "I don't know. What?"

"The Red-Haired Siren Clan reported a band of strangers near Blue Lake."

"Ohhh? Are they highway men?" Flax could hear the excitement in the little demoness' voice. It reminded him of a tot having just been promised a pony.

"Maybe. If they are, they're all yours to play with. But that's for tomorrow. Now it's bedtime!"

Deep in the shadows, peeking around the trunk of the tree, he saw Gretchen lean forward and kiss the demonic girl's forehead. Whereupon she squealed, popped up and streaked out into the hall like a watermelon seed beneath a thumbnail.

His blood suddenly ran cold when, despite the distance and the shadows, Gretchen turned towards him and looked directly into his eyes. He felt frozen in place as she said,

"Please be a good boy and there'll be a fresh bowl of sweet cream for you by the kitchen door every night." Then, she stood and turned, pausing only momentarily to say over her shoulder, "Good night, Flax."

But he had bounded away the instant she turned her back to him and was too distant to hear.
***
If you want to learn more about the Darke Family and their world, please follow the Selene Darke Series. Book One: Almost Darke is available in ebook and paperback. Book Two is due out in 2022.

P..J. Black

Lois Thompson Bartholomew made her first writing sale in 1979, a parenting tip that sold for $10. Houghton Mifflin Harcourt bought her first novel The White Dove. It is republished as an ebook, a paperback, and an audiobook available at books2read.com/ltbart and https://shop.authors-direct.com and ttps://www.loisthompsonbartholomew.com/ She is a member of SCBWI and TAF.

Rush Hour

The cars are doing their commuter dance.
Do-si-do,
Stop and go.
Turn right on the red,
Turn left on the green.
Speed up, slow down,
Pass in between.
Enter and merge,
Exit, slow down.
Go fast on the left
Slow traffic keep right.
No trucks in this lane.
The rest in between.
Do-si-do,
Stop and go.
The cars are doing their commuter dance.

The Cloak

It was just an old cloak—the kind you see people wearing in those movies. You know, the kind of cloak people wore to escape from Paris and the guillotine during the French revolution. It had a hood, of course, so a lady could hide her hair and her face, if she pulled it forward enough. A man could wear it too. And if he carried a scythe he'd look like the grim reaper on Halloween

It looked like it probably belonged to a man. I mean, it was huge, big enough to completely cover a tall man with broad shoulders. At least, that was what I thought the first time I pulled it out of that old dresser in Grandma's attic. I pulled it out and held it up to me and almost half of it puddled on the floor. I heard that Grandpa was a big man.

But Grandma was no petite little girl, either. Ma said Grandma and Grandpa matched up like a pair of twins. He had her by a couple of inches, but, yep, that cloak could have been hers, too. Me, I take after my ma. She was little and petite. And me? Well, my friends used to call me "runt," and if I made some of the gang members in the neighborhood mad, they called me a "skinny runt," along with other things that I don't like to write down. Grandma always said I still had some growth left in me, and that my muscles would bulk up some day. But so far that someday hadn't come. And that cloak was definitely too big for me.

Right then I wasn't sure if I was going to wear the cloak when I left or just take the car. So, I just tossed it on the back of that old rocking chair that Grandma used to keep down in the kitchen when she was alive. She liked to sit down after the dishes were done at night and rock and read. It reminded me too much of her after she died, so I hauled it up into the attic and put it there by that old dresser.

Well, by the end of the next week my mind was made up. I had to leave, and I decided I liked the idea of using the cloak instead of the car. I loved this neighborhood when I was a kid. People up and down the block on both sides of the street always said, "hi" and "How're ya' doin'?" And they cared.

They really did care. But not anymore. Most of those old families are gone. The ones with kids moved out to find better schools where there wasn't so much bad stuff going on.

The old folks like Grandma...well they just died off. Their grown-up children cleaned out their houses and then put them up for sale. But it's hard to sell houses in this neighborhood. Some of them have been empty for 5 years or more. Get a few empty houses with yards full of long grass and flower beds just a mess of weeds, and squatters start to move in.

At first, we tried to make friends with these new people, at least Grandma did. But she soon saw that being friendly branded her as a soft touch and pretty soon it seemed like every person in the block wanted to stop by and borrow something. They said "borrow," but what they really meant was "steal." Then Grandma died and I knew I'd have to make up my mind.

I'd heard stories about that cloak since before I could walk. Seems like everyone in the family, Ma, Pa, Grandma, the uncles and aunts and great-uncles, and great-aunts, all had stories about the cloak. My cousins and I loved to listen to the stories, but not one of those who really knew about it, or at least said they knew about it, seemed to know where it was. But when I was about ten, I started to notice something.

When we kids asked to see the cloak, all the grownups said they had no idea what happened to it. All but one. Grandma never said that. I don't think the others noticed, but I did. When questions about the cloak got too specific, Grandma would find an excuse to go do something — get Aunt Lorna a glass of water, or go let the dog out or something. So, I figured she was the one person who did know where it was.

Still, thinking about using the cloak scared me. But by a month after the funeral, I was desperate. I tried to act normal and even kept going to school most days. At least Grandma had made me go get my driver's license as soon as I was old enough. She did all she could to make things easy for me. She paid all the bills a couple of months ahead. She kept adding to her store of emergency food until the basement looked like a grocery store.

"This will keep you going for a little while," she told me one day while I stacked cans of Chicken Noodle Soup on the shelves. "But you do know you have to leave after I'm gone. Don't stay here. It isn't safe any longer. Those gangs from across the freeway are starting to move over here."

Then she came right up in my face. "Now you listen to me. Do not stay here after I'm gone."

I promised over and over I'd leave. But where? Where would I go?

I asked Grandma more than once. "That has to be your choice," she said. "Where and when have to come from you. Just don't forget your history lessons."

I thought she was just stringing her words together strange, but after I found her letter, I realized what she was saying.

A couple of weeks after the funeral I decided I'd better start getting things together. I wanted to find that cloak. I kept searching Grandma's bedroom but it wasn't there. Finally, I just decided to pack some stuff to be ready to leave, even without the cloak. I drug my backpack, the one I used on camping trips, out from the back of my closet and dumped it on my bed to see what I'd left in there from our last camping trip. That was over a year before, so I grabbed the stale granola bars, tossed them in the trash and threw away a couple of pairs of dirty socks that never did make it to the wash.

Then I saw the letter. The white envelope stood out from the rest of the stuff and I saw my name, written in Grandma's handwriting, on the front, Mr. Caleb Alexander Graham. Grandma and everyone else just called me Alex. When Grandma used my full name, I knew I'd better sit up and take notice. I ripped it open.

"Dear Alex,"

"I wish I could help you today, but I can't. Always know I love you. Pack the small album of family photos from the drawer in my nightstand. Take the packet of documents in the sealed plastic envelope, also in the drawer in my nightstand. Your birth certificate is in there and other important papers. The cloak is in the bottom drawer of the dresser in the back corner of the attic. Under it is the history book I read to you when you were little. Be sure to take it.

You need to decide where you want to go. The history book is the only guide connected to the cloak. You need them both or neither one will work.

"Put on your backpack, decide on a place, and a time, then put on the cloak and hang on. You know what else to take. Wear hiking boots, two or three pairs of socks, a couple of layers of clothes, a heavy sweatshirt or sweater, your jacket and a knit winter hat. Put a change of nice clothes and some lighter shoes in the backpack with your underwear and dried food. Don't forget a flashlight, extra batteries, your Swiss Army knife, a full canteen and your first-aid kit.

"And be sure to take the coin purse. I put it in an inside pocket of the cloak. Always keep it there so you have the kind of money you need. It will change depending on where you are. Be careful where you go and what time you choose. Read everything about whatever place you decide to visit.

"All my love, Grandma"

Right away I ran upstairs and this time I found the cloak. Once I saw it and held it up to me, I couldn't see how I could wear it without stumbling over it, but it was all I had. I felt the coin purse in the pocket. I folded Grandma's letter up small and put it in there too. But then I just tossed the cloak on that chair and went down stairs, taking the history book with me.

I decided to go ahead and get ready so I found all the stuff Grandma mentioned in her letter and packed. The layers of clothes and socks, my hiking boots and jacket and stuff I laid out on the bed in Ma's old room. The food I stacked up in the corner of the kitchen counter. I kept changing that pile, eating some and then adding more. But there was plenty to choose from without having to go to the store. I ate as much of the stuff in the freezer as I could, especially the three boxes of ice cream bars.

The last day I went to school, a guy from my street, one of the ones who had "borrowed" stuff from Grandma, knocked into me in the hall. At first, I was mad. Then I walked outside. It was cold so I put my hands in my pockets. I felt a piece of paper in the right-hand pocket. I dashed back into the warmth of the school, turned my back on the kids streaming out the door and opened it up. This kid hardly ever talked in class unless the teacher made him, and he wrote like he talked, short. I read his note twice and my stomach twisted until I thought I'd throw up.

"Get out before midnight. It's your turn tonight."

105

I knew right away what he meant. Once a month, the night of the full moon, a bunch of the new move-ins raided a house in the neighborhood. Mostly they took stuff, but if anyone still lived there, that person usually ended up in the hospital afterward. They came home to a wreck of a house. I had helped some of the people clean up after raids. I didn't want to be around to even see our house in the morning.

I took off, went straight home and drove directly into the garage and shut the garage door. Then I grabbed my backpack full of school books and ran inside. The first thing I did was check the locks on all the doors and windows and close the curtains. I had about four hours before dark. I looked around in Grandma's room to see if I missed anything. Nope.

I had saved one ice cream bar for my going away supper. So, I wolfed down a peanut butter and jelly sandwich and then got the ice cream bar out to eat. My stomach was so tight I didn't know if I could finish it, but I did. I tried to enjoy it, but by then I just wanted to be gone.

I went to Ma's room and dressed. I waddled more than walked after putting on three pairs of jeans plus three shirts, the hoodie I chose over the sweater, and my jacket. I stuck my toboggan on my head. (That's what we call those warm knit hats. I found out later that most people think a toboggan is a long sled.) I zipped my gloves and pocket knife into the pockets of my jacket and I was almost ready. I went to my room and got my backpack, double checking that I had the clothes and shoes, the photo album and the legal papers.

Then I went to the kitchen and finished filling the backpack with the food I had stacked up. I didn't have room for it all, so I put the jerky and some granola bars in my pockets, then grabbed a package of cinnamon bears and stuffed it between the layers of my shirts.

Picking up the history book I climbed the stairs to the attic. I still didn't know where to go. I had intended to sit down one night and really read the history book, but this just all came too sudden. So now I sat down on the rocking chair and opened the book. I thought I'd look at places out west. One entry caught my eye.

"At the turn of the century, San Francisco was the Queen of the West. A more vibrant city could not be found. Gateway to the Orient and the islands of the Pacific Ocean, it was a hub of culture, finance and trade."

There was more, but I didn't bother to turn the page. I wanted to get out of there and didn't even think that in her letter Grandma said "Read everything about whatever place you decide to visit." No, "San Francisco, Queen of the West," sounded like the place for me. Even a sixteen- year-old ought to be able to find a job in a place like that. I didn't really have a date in mind, but my birthday was April 17, so that's the day I picked. And the year? I wasn't so sure about that. Then I remembered that 1906 was an important year for San Francisco for some reason, so that's the year I put in my mind.

I shrugged into the backpack and after letting the belt out all the way I managed to snap it shut over all my clothes. I picked up the cloak. It was getting dark and I was so jumpy by now I wasn't even really surprised when I put the cloak on and found it fit me perfectly. It came just to the top of my hiking boots and completely covered me and all my stuff. I picked up the history book, held it tight, and thought of San Francisco, April 17, 1906.

I should have turned the page. (I really wished I had turned the page).

At 5:12 a.m. On Wednesday, April 18, 1906 a major earthquake struck San Francisco and the Northern California coast. Even more deadly than the earthquake itself were the fires which broke out all over the city, burning for days. Although local officials tried to minimize the death toll in official reports, estimates place it at nearly 3000 people. Over 80% of San Francisco was destroyed.

Lois Thompson Bartholomew

Erika V. Hoffman has fiction publ. in Deadly Ink Anthologies, Tough Lit. Magazine, and Page & Spine and Why Mama after it won First Place in a contest. Erika's stories appear in Chicken Soup for the Soul and Sasee among other publications. Her published stories are formatted into books.

Cookie and Chip and Spandex

Athena told her mom she didn't have time to deliver Tollhouse cookies to the USO at the airport. She had a biochemistry test to cram for and shadowing duties with a dentist at the university. After all, she hadn't volunteered for the cookie drop off; she hadn't joined the DAR; she wasn't sure how she felt about war. Besides, her mother probably only imagined she was coming down with the Swine Flu. If her mom heard about some ailment by talking heads on TV, within five minutes she'd develop all the symptoms. Weeks had passed since Athena's episode with H1N1.

"Aren't you afraid of spreading the epidemic by baking cookies?" Athena asked.

"I washed my hands," her mom replied.

"Tsk! You don't have the virus." She swatted the air dismissing her mom's claims.

"How do you know?"

"You don't have HIN cause you wouldn't be standing upright arguing with me!" Athena huffed to the car and balanced the five boxes as she fumbled for the Land Rover's key. Her mother followed obsequiously. Athena muttered, "I should be studying. You nag me to get into dental school next fall but then chew up my time doing stupid chores like this one! I bet you'll fiddle around with your computer and probably scribble some lame story for some stupid, shmaltzy anthology you submit to, while I'm doing your errand!" She slammed the car door, backed up, and squealed away.

"Darn it! I forgot my GPS." Athena slapped the steering wheel. She knew the way but hadn't paid attention to her mother's instructions.

Her mom had mumbled something about a cardboard sign in a window. Athena couldn't recall which terminal provided the USO service. She scoured her memory but remembered only her mom, in pink fuzzy slippers, waving a tissue and saying, "Remember to thank the troops for serving! Be nice! You may be one of their last memories. Of home," she'd added.

As Athena zoomed up to the terminal, she craned her neck looking for the USO sign. She slowed. A security officer officiously gestured for her to move on.

"All right, Bubba," she murmured. When has a terrorist ever bombed a car loading or unloading passengers? Heck, I'll park and go inside and ask someone where to go.

She swerved into a space nearly plowing over a woman pushing her elderly father in a wheelchair. The caregiver threw her a harsh look. Athena lip-synched:

"Sorry."

She hopped out, sprinted to the passenger door, and hoisted the boxes up, but couldn't see over them. They wobbled.

Athena pivoted. She dropped them Pell-Mell onto the seat. She screamed inwardly. She'd have to go inside and ask for help.

Because she'd planned on stopping by her professor's office to solicit a recommendation, Athena had dressed in stockings and heels instead of her usual jeans and

Northface jacket. Her hound tooth suit seemed uber –
professional, and her auburn hair tied back in a knot at the
nape of her neck looked classy, too. A hint of mascara, a
dab of blush, and clear lip gloss (instead of the Egyptian
maquillage she adorned herself with when she and her gal
pals frequented the bar hopping scene) was all the make-up
she wore.

At 22, she found drinking passé. She mused about
how much more fun getting hammered had been when
underage with a fake ID.

Athena started to feel old her last semester of
college. Living at home during college had contained
benefits but mostly liabilities. She longed for her own
apartment where she could entertain a guy, in privacy.

She hustled through the suitcase-laden crowd and
approached a sky hop. The black man smiled broadly at the
pretty co-ed. "Hep you, ma'am?"

"I'm looking for a USO rep."

"Yes, ma'am. Go through the automatic doors. Turn
right. Ask the lady at information to call up there."

Athena smiled beatifically and murmured thanks.
She gritted her teeth as she glimpsed her watch. Time was
slipping away. Unfortunately, the information gal was
yakking on the phone. When she saw Athena approach, she
lowered her eyes.

"Ahem!" Athena uttered and coughed. She shifted
her weight. She steadied both fists on the counter. "EXCUSE
ME! I'm here to deliver cookies to the USO!"

The yakker blinked, covered the receiver, nodded,
and whispered, "I'll call Joe." Athena sighed deeply. The
woman hissed into the phone, "Hold on." She pressed line
2.

"A young lady's here, Joe, with cookies for soldiers." She looked up at Athena. "Miss, are you from the DAR?"

"Yes."

"She is, Joe. Okay. I'll tell her." The woman pressed down the button. "Joe will be right down. You can have a seat over there." She gestured to a line of chairs against massive windows where one frazzled woman with a dozen frisky kids sat in agony.

"Thanks, I'll stand," replied Athena whose heels tapped the floor as she paced while she consulted her Rolex. Five minutes passed. A stooped old man hobbled up. His red vest read USO. He held out his hand; his eyes crinkled.

"Why, Miss. I'm sorry to keep you waiting. I'm Joe Short. You've the cookies from the DAR?"

"They're in the car."

"Want to pull around?"

"Can't someone meet me at my car? I have an appointment to make. I'm just doin' a favor for my mom." The words tumbled out in machine gun chatter.

"Certainly."

Athena studied the old man. "There are five large containers. Send someone strong."

"Will do!" He yelled as he limped off.

"I'm parked in 15B. A Land Rover. Gun metal gray."

Joe nodded and made a thumbs-up sign.

Athena cursed herself for agreeing to this mission. She swore her mother was inconsiderate of her time. Rushing to her car, she grabbed her cell phone from her Juicy Couture bag and dialed her professor.

"Come on, answer!" she ordered.

"Doctor Sokolof speaking"

"This is Athena Tucker."

"Yes?"

"I've an appointment with you today at 2:00."

"Yes."

"It's 1:45, but I'm stuck at the airport."

"Oh?"

"I'm not going anywhere. I'm delivering cookies to the USO.

"This concerns me—how?"

"Ah, ah, um… I might be late."

He cleared his throat. "I see,"

"How about 2:30?" she said anxiously.

"You're still at the airport?"

"About to leave."

"I have another appointment. Check back next week."

"But I need…"

"Goodbye, Miss Tucker."

"Drat!" she yelled. She slammed the phone against her head. I bet he's liberal. Why did I mention the USO? Stupid, stupid me! Then, it occurred to her she could make her date with the prof if she sped to the campus right now. She'd barge in his office and exclaim: "Made it on time after all!" It was doable.

She'd leave the cookies on the curb in front of the parking space. Surely, the USO volunteer would find them; she'd attach a note to them. Athena located an old receipt from her purse and penned: "Bon Appétit! From your local DAR Chapter; thanks for your service."

Athena hoisted the onerous containers out of the car. They slid back and forth as she tottered on her high heels. She couldn't see over them. One crashed to the pavement. She shifted her weight to prevent more from falling but tripped over the cement divider between her space and the

one in front of her car. She toppled to the ground with the
boxes. One opened. Baked goodies spewed forth.

Like a rag doll tossed haphazardly among cardboard
refuse in a recycling center, she lay. Her taupe stockings
tore at the knee; blood seeped through a nasty gash.
Mascara-hued tears tumbled. She gazed at her chipped
French-styled fingernails, smudged jacket, and sprained
ankle. Covering her face with her hands, she gave way to
sobs.

Suddenly from behind, two large hands grabbed her
under her armpits and heaved her up.

"Let me have a look." A soldier peered at her knee.
He fell to his knees and jerked out a handkerchief and
applied pressure to stem the flow. She gazed down at the top
of his beret. He didn't look up but held the hankie tight to
her gash.

"Thanks."

"It's abating," he replied not raising his head.

"Thank you… for your service," she said with a lilt,
remembering her mom's instructions.

"No problem, Ma'am." The man straightened, all 6
feet 2 inches of him. Athena went from looking at the top of
his head to gazing up at the chiseled jaw of a handsome
Marine. His glacier blue eyes pulsated with brightness. His
perfect white teeth and tempting mouth dazzled her.

"The cookies…" she gestured to the forlorn boxes.

"No problem," he repeated. He collected the boxes,
refilling the empty one with the cookies that had escaped.

"Let me put them in your vehicle until you're
patched up."

She clicked open the hatchback. He assembled the
boxes in the corner of the back and hustled over to her.

"Put your arm around my neck. Use me as a crutch."
He opened the door to the back seat. "Let's elevate your leg

114

a few minutes." He reclined her and slid into the other side.

Gently, he held her swollen ankle and massaged it. Occasionally, he'd dab at her wound with his bloodied hankie.

"I'm supposed to be helping you guys by delivering these cookies. Here, I'm the one in need of help." She forced a weak smile.

"A damsel in distress?" He winked.

"More than you know!"

He shot a wry look at her. "How's that?"

"I was supposed to meet with this ass of a professor today. I need him to write a good rec. That's why I dressed like this! Usually, I wear tattered jeans and flip-flops."

"I thought you spruced up for us. To give us soldiers a vision to dream about when we're in Afghanistan."

"You're deployed there?"

"My plane's in five hours."

Athena became mum. He pulled on each of her toes.

"They call this reflexology. Pulling toes costs big bucks at fancy spas." He grinned. "How am I doing?"

She laughed. "The ER would charge a lot to treat this gash."

'True."

"Say!" He tilted his head in a flirty way. "What if I charge you something, Ma'am?"

"What?"

"A couple of cookies. Let's wipe off the stragglers and eat them!" He reached back for those that had topped out earlier.

"You're not afraid of germs?" she asked, as he brushed off specks.

"Honey, I'll be in raghead territory tomorrow. I'll be breathing and eating dirt." He handed her the cleanest one after inspecting a few. He popped two in his mouth. She bit

115

into one. The chocolate chips oozed out and resided in the corners of her lips. He reached his finger over and wiped the chocolate from them.

"You're beautiful," he said. She closed her eyes and moved her head imperceptibly closer. "May I kiss you?" he asked.

She gulped hard, swallowing the rest of the cookie. She had a boyfriend. She opened her eyes, and his wide honest-looking face leaned towards hers. He lay her ankle down softly. He crouched over her.

"May I?" She felt a tingling. Warmth filled her body with a twinge of excitement.

"Beautiful girl, I don't want to sound morose, but this may be the last kiss I get for…awhile."

"Just one kiss?" she asked. He nodded affirmatively. She shut her eyes. He swooped down, and his mouth grappled with hers. He bit her lips. He held her head tight.

He slid his lips all over her trembling ones and down her neck and behind her ear and left a trail of wetness as he retraced his kissing up to her closed eyelids and grazed each of them and then licked her face back to her mouth where he inserted his tongue. Vigorously, he worked it around her mouth as he clutched her in a no holds barred death grip. He pushed his muscular chest against her bosom, and she felt limp and…willing. He finally backed off her mouth and slid the wisps of her loosened hair into her love knot behind her ears, and his hot breath in her ears seemed to announce: "Again." Her brown eyes streaked in black gazed into the bluest sky eyes she'd ever seen.

"You want another kiss?" she asked.

"Kiss me back."

She parted her lips, and he plunged. He sucked her lips and murmured and groaned as he began another long kiss. His hands came to rest on a button.

"May I?" he breathed.

Every fiber of her screamed yes. Every pore cried out: "More." Every scintilla of her brain wanted him now, maybe forever. She stared at him and said, "No."

"NO?" Bitter disappointment raced over his features.

"Yes."

"Yes?" He repeated hopeful.

"NO! I mean yes, the answer's no."

"I see." He sat up suddenly. He seemed aloof. He pressed his eyes closed grappling with composure. The windows had steamed over. He couldn't see out. "I'd better get the cookies delivered," he announced.

'Uh-huh." Athena straightened up to a sitting position. She re-buttoned her top button and smoothed down her jacket.

He bit his lip as he contemplated her. "Give me your arm," he said.

Leary, she extended it. He pulled out a ballpoint pen and pressed it hard on her flesh, writing. Then, he put her hand back in her lap. "A little tattoo: My contact info. If you want me, you'll know how to reach me."

She stretched out her arm and saw the e-mail, the phone number, and a street and city address. "You live in Idaho?"

"Been there?" he asked.

"Never."

"You'll like it."

"Will I?"

"I'd bet my life on it."

117

Her eyes watered. "Take care of yourself, Soldier Boy."

He jumped out of the car, marched around to the back, collected the cookies, and smiled.

"Till then, Cookie."

She slipped outside the car with her fingers on the handle to the driver's side...

"Till then, Chip."

"Write, maybe?"

"Do I look like a kiss- and- run type?"

He cocked his head to the side and studied her memorizing her features, her body, her stance.

"You look like the unforgettable type."

"I won't forget."

He laid down the boxes, put his arms around her, and hugged her to his chest in a farewell embrace.

"Same place, same time, next year," he said.

"The airport parking lot?"

"You'll recognize me?"

"You have one of those common faces, I dunno," she mocked. "All Marines look alike. I might grope the wrong guy."

He tilted back his head and laughed. "The unforgettable type," he said.

"How will I spot you?"

"The unforgettable type," he repeated robotically.

"I won't forget you, either."

"Same place, same time, next year," he said, again.

"A rendezvous in the airport parking lot? Hmm that's not too romantic. Security cameras, you know."

"There are none." He smiled strangely. "Believe me I know. I've been assured that..."

"You know? What you've done this before? Picked up girls in airport parking lots a regular thing for you?" She laughed coquettishly. He titled back his head and laughed a throaty laugh.

"Bye, now," she said teasingly with a lilt. She batted her eyes, feeling the swoon of love.

"Close your eyes, Sweetheart. It's better for you---if you close your eyes."

He smiled tightly and then pulled the twine out of his pocket and with one fell swoop, looped it around her neck. As her eyes bulged and she gasped for air, he opened the door and put her gently down on the seat. It didn't take long to turn her into a limp doll.

"Tease," he hissed and spat on her face. Then, tucking the twine back into his pocket, he strode out of the parking lot quickly only pausing to give a rigid salute to an old man in a red vest accompanied by a real Marine. The killer's lips twitched with a tinge of sadistic delight as he rounded the corner and disappeared into a waiting elevator.

As the doors closed, his head fell back, and he unzipped an entire body suit. He laughed with his perfectly straight white teeth until he unhinged the head with Tom Brady chin.

"Idaho," he chortled. "Does it even exist?" An otherworldly being with one large eye and a gooey layer of membranes stared down at the floor of the elevator where lay the human spandex suit in marine uniform.

"I'm getting Alzheimer's Disease," stooped Joe Short remarked to the dark–eyed, Hispanic Marine by his side. "I was dang sure that young lass told me the parking lot in Terminal One, not this one in Terminal Two. I hope we're not too late. She was an impatient young thing. She might have scooted off. Pretty, though. Very pretty. You'll see. Maybe she's still here; it's got to be fifteen minutes passed."

Erika V. Hoffman

Patricia "Pat" Bumpass is author of Jump into Creativity, a freelance content creator for small businesses, and coach who encourages and empowers women of color to lean into their true authentic selves by engaging in self-care. She is the creator of beautiful, motivational 44-card decks that inspire. They're great for women writers! Learn more at www.patriciabumpass.com

Splintered Heart

"What's got you so upset?" asks Darius as I hang my keys and purse on the peg inside the front door of our two-bedroom apartment. Rather than acknowledge him or his question, I go into our bedroom to prepare for bed. Darius watches me take off my makeup from the bathroom door. I see in the mirror he's loosened his tie. He walks to his sink and brushes his teeth while tracking my every move.

I finish up and climb into bed. He turns the light off in the bathroom and settles into his side. "I guess we're not talking about whatever's bothering you?" In response, I turn my back to him and turn out my light. He sighs and readjusts himself on the bed, then turns so he can do the same to the light on his side of the bed.

The next morning, I'm sitting at the table when Darius enters the kitchen. He leans down for a kiss. "Good morning, beautiful." I turn my cheek to him.

He sighs, pours himself a cup of coffee, and takes his seat across from me. "Are we finally going to discuss what upset you last night?"

I look at him. "You seriously don't know what you did or, in this case, didn't do last night at dinner?"

"If I knew, I wouldn't be asking."

"What did that obnoxious man say about me in front of the entire table?" At his blank look, I continue. "He said, 'Is that going to be enough for you, big girl?' while I was placing my order. Throughout the entire meal, he made a comment every time I raised my fork to my mouth."

"Babe, he was drunk and, like you said, obnoxious and rude. Nobody paid any attention to what came out of his mouth."

"So, it was ok for him to act that way toward the woman you profess to love?"

"I'm not saying that, but I think you're blowing this way out of proportion."

"Blowing it out of proportion." I repeat. "You were nothing but cordial with every lady at our table. Why wouldn't you expect the other men seated at the table to be cordial to me?"

"I didn't want to cause a scene by getting into it with him inside the restaurant. Besides, I knew you'd handle it."

"You didn't want to cause a scene in the restaurant? What about in the parking lot? They parked right next to us. Let me guess, you didn't want to cause a scene there either. Was I supposed to sit there and let him talk down to me all night? You weren't saying anything. Hell, yes, I handled it. "

I get up and put my cup in the sink with enough force that it shatters. Darius is at my side in an instant, trying to staunch the flow of blood. "Let me see." He pulls down the first aid kit we keep on top of the refrigerator.

Wrapping my hand in a towel, I turn away from him. "You didn't care enough last night to defend me. Don't worry about a minor cut this morning."

He grabs my hand and removes the towel. "Come on Rayne, that cut looks deep. Hold still so I can try to stop the bleeding."

As soon as he bandages my finger, I step away from him, grab my briefcase, and head toward the door. "I won't be here for dinner with your mom. Please make my apologies."

"Rayne…" I hear him call as I close the front door.

***

I'm sitting at my desk in the graphic design firm I own nestled in the heart of downtown, staring at the wall of my office when my assistant sticks her head in the door. "Boss, Darius' mom is on line one."

I look up at her for a moment. "Please let Kaye know I'm on my way to a meeting out of the office and will be gone for the rest of the day." She nods her head and leaves.

After a few minutes, she returns. "Boss, is everything alright? You've been staring at the wall since you got here."

Ignoring her question, I say, "Lisa, why don't we close shop for the rest of the day? You can go home to spend some quality time with your husband and that precious baby."

She smiles. "I'll take you up on that offer. But don't think you're off the hook. Tomorrow, I expect breakfast and a long conversation about what's got you so bothered." She waits until I look up and nod. "Want to walk out together?"

"Sure. I'll forward my phones to your line, and you can change your voicemail."

Ten minutes later, we've gathered our things and exit the building. As we're walking out the door, I hear my name called. "Rayne Amana." Leaning against the side of the building just out of sight is Darius' mom.

Lisa asks, "Want me to run interference, boss lady?"

I shake my head. "Thanks Lisa. I'm good. Kiss that cute baby boy of yours for me. See you tomorrow."

When I turn to face her again, Kaye has stepped closer. "I'm glad I caught you. Walk with me to that cute little bistro, Gracie's. They have the best tuna melts and homemade chips. Their blueberry iced tea is to die for. Surely you have time for a quick bite before your meeting." She hooks her hand in the crook of my arm.

The minute we walk in the door, my step falters as the smells assault me.

"Are you okay, dear? You've gone ashen."

I swallow. "Yeah. I need to use the restroom. I'll be right back." Before she can protest, I dash off. Inside the bathroom stall, I place my head against the cold tile of the wall while my stomach settles.

Kaye secures a table for us in a secluded corner of the back terrace. Once we've placed our orders and the waiter brings our drinks, she starts in with the reason for visiting me at my office.

"Honey, be honest. You were trying to avoid me, weren't you?" At my blank look, she waves her hand in dismissal. It's okay, sweetheart. You don't have to answer. Let me just say you and Darius have been together for four years. You've never missed a weekly dinner, yet he tells me you won't be with us tonight."

I take a sip of water to give myself a minute to collect my thoughts. "I'm sorry. Is there a question in there?"

This woman, who could be Dianne Carroll's twin, places her chin on her interlaced fingers. "Do not play coy with me, young lady. You know perfectly well that I am asking you why?"

"That's between Darius and me."

The waiter chooses that moment to bring our food. As soon as he leaves, she's at it again. "Be that as it may, I want to know what has happened that is so bad you find it unpleasant to spend this evening with me."

"It has nothing to do with you. Trust me."

"It affects me. I suppose it has never occurred to you I put up with my insufferable son once a week because I get to see you. You're the daughter I never had."

I look down at my food, then sigh before launching into the events of the previous evening. When I'm finished, Kaye stares at me before saying, "My son did not take after his father. Phillip would have punched that man. Come on, let's get you home. I have a bone to pick with him."

While she's paying the check, she dials her son's number. I hear him when he answers. "Did you talk to Rayne?"

"I did. Drop whatever you're doing right this minute and meet us at your place… I don't care. Family is more important than some deadline." She ends the call.

At our apartment building, we park in the underground deck and go up to wait for Darius, who has further to travel. When he comes in, I'm sitting at the kitchen table drinking a cup of tea. I don't look at him when he enters.

Kaye doesn't give him a chance to greet her. She pulls out a chair. "Sit."

He looks at me across the table. "You told my mama?"

Finally, looking up at him, I answer, "You started this. Besides, she accosted me at my work."

She interrupts, "You didn't tell me Darius because you knew I would side with Rayne. The man's job is to protect his woman. No. Matter. What. If you learned nothing else from your dad, I would have hoped it was how to treat a lady - especially one who has stood by you during some of

124

the darkest days of your life. From what I hear, you didn't do that."

Kaye looks at her son and puts her purse on her shoulder. "I'm cancelling tonight's dinner. You were wrong, Darius. Now fix it. Think about who and what is slipping through your fingers." She walks over to me and kisses me on the forehead. "Let me know how things go." I swallow and nod.

After she closes the door, Darius reaches across the table to grasp my hand. "You took the bandage off."

"It stopped bleeding, so..." I shrug. We sit there, neither of us saying anything. Darius runs his hands across his bald head before standing up to remove his suit jacket. I track his every move. "You don't see why I'm so upset, do you?"

"I should have said something to that guy last night. But you handled it yourself."

"Because you didn't." I sigh.

"My mom is right. Dad would have punched his lights out. I always promised myself I wouldn't be like him. He was overprotective of mama one minute and making plans to meet one of his women the next. He took me with him when mom was at work or had a temple meeting. He wasn't the best example in that respect, but he protected what was his."

"We've already discussed what would happen if I found you cheating on me. But I expect you to take up for me when I'm being attacked - physically, mentally, emotionally."

He squats down in front of me. "There is nothing I can do about it now, so can we please put it behind us?" He looks up at me with wide-eyed innocence.

I lean down and kiss the top of his head as I sniff back the tears threatening to break free. "Get up. I need to go to the bathroom." At our bedroom door, I place my hand on his chest. He wraps his around mine and brings it to his lips. The tears roll down my face.

When I come out if our bedroom, I sit my bag by the front door. Darius gets up from his seat in the living room.

"Where are you going?"

"I'm going to go stay with my parents until I decide my next steps."

"Next steps? This is that serious to you? I could see if I slept with someone else, but I didn't." Without saying a word, I walk towards the door. Darius grabs my wrist.

"You're not leaving me." I yank my arm away and stumble into the wall. I double over and grab my stomach.

"Come on Rayne. You couldn't have hit the wall that hard." He steps toward me the instant before my world goes black. I have the sensation of slipping to the floor.
***

I wake up and look around. My parents and Kaye are on one side of my bed. Darius is sitting in a chair next to me on the other side, holding my hand. I swallow and lick my lips.

"What happened?"

He kisses my hand and looks at me with tears in his eyes. "I thought I'd lost you. You had an incomplete miscarriage. The doctors did a D & C. They said you've been bleeding for at least a day. Why didn't you tell me?"

"When can I leave?" I ask after licking my lips and extricating my hand from Darius'.

Mom takes my hand and says, "The doctors want to keep you for observation tonight. You lost a lot of blood."

Kaye steps forward and says, Darius why don't you and Mr. Amana go get us some sandwiches?" After they leave, my mom pulls up a chair while Kaye takes the one vacated by

Darius. She picks up my other hand. "You knew you were miscarrying at the bistro, didn't you?"

I cast my eyes down, then nod my head. I cover my eyes to staunch the flood of tears threatening to overtake me. Mom squeezes my hand. "Honey, you were supposed to be taking it easy. Your doctor told you the least amount of stress could cause you to miscarry. What happened?"

"It doesn't matter, mom. I spent all day trying to keep my heart from splitting in two. For the baby, if not for myself. I was going to tell Darius last night after dinner. But that didn't work out."

"One thing I know for sure is my son loves you very much."

"Thank you for that Kaye. Sometimes love isn't enough." I look at my mom. "When I'm discharged, I want to stay with you and Dad until I'm back on my feet. I'll plan on staying in the apartment above my office after that." Mom blinks back tears. "You can stay with us for as long as you need to. What about Darius?"

Kaye looks at me. "She's leaving him. Make no mistake. I love my son dearly. But I did not raise him to be this stupid. His father cheated on me with anything in a skirt, but he always protected me - especially from bullies. I'm so sorry you feel this is your only recourse. Do you think therapy will help?"

"The wounds are too deep. Add this on top of all the things neither of you knows about and I'm going to need some time. Mom, will you call Lisa and let her know she's going to need to handle things for a few days?"

"Of course, dear." She goes off to a corner to make the call.

I look at Darius' mom. "I have one request."

"Anything."

127

"Take Darius home. He's going to want to stay, but I don't have the energy to deal with him tonight. In fact, all of you can go home. I'll be fine."

The guys return with the food. Everybody sticks around to eat with me. When Kaye notices that I'm picking at my sandwich, she clears her throat. "I think it's time we all left Rayne to get some rest. Including you, Darius."

"No mom. I'm staying right here."

I look at him and sigh. "Darius, I don't want you to stay. And when I'm discharged, I'll go home with my mom and dad for a few days."

Darius looks at me with tears in his eyes. "When you're discharged, you should sleep in your own bed. I'll move some of my things into mom's until you decide what you want to do about…" He swallows and looks at his feet. When he looks back at me, his eyes beseech me. "Don't give up on us. Give me a chance to grieve with you and prove I am the man for you."

He kisses me one last time. "I love you." Without another word, he walks out the door. Kaye kisses my forehead, then follows her son.

My parents leave with a promise to be back early the next morning. Ready to take me home and into my new life, where I can pick up the pieces of my splintered heart.

Patricia "Pat" Bumpass

Terri DeGezelle Michels, author and photographer, has published more than 60 children's non-fiction titles. Her newest title, Simon of Cyrene, the Legend of the Easter Egg published by Pauline Books and Media. Terri shares her writing experiences during school visits, encouraging children to follow their dream.

In Good Hands

"Need a little help?"

Great, that's all I need a busybody next door watching me, I thought. I glanced up from assessing my freshly hammered thumb and saw a man leap over the three-foot back yard fence and stroll over to me.

"Was it my scream or just the way I was using the hammer that gave me away?" I asked with my voice trembling. I kept my eyes cast downward, careful not to let this newcomer see tears threatening to spill over. My injured thumb represented one more way I had failed at doing things for myself.

"I think it was a combination of the hurt, animal-like howl and the flying hammer that gave you away," he replied.

"You are very intuitive," I said, before sticking my throbbing thumb in my mouth, trying to suck away the hurt like a two-year-old child.

"Instead of an offer of help, maybe I should be asking you if you need a new thumb."

Looking at the pair of, size 13, sandaled feet in front of me, I lifted my head, taking in a handsome, athletic specimen of a man. Twinkling chocolate brown eyes met mine.

"May I properly introduce myself?" Without waiting for my reply, he added, "Peter, Peter Warner. I moved in last

week." Reaching out his right hand then pulling it back as quickly, he
shook his head and said, "Sorry, maybe when that thumb quits throbbing." His heart-warming smile almost made me forget the pain.

I offered my left hand. "Here, this one doesn't hurt. I'm Emma. I meant to stop over with a plate of cookies, but it seems you beat me to the introduction."

Holding my hand in his, he said, "It's nice to meet you, Emma. I'm sorry about your thumb. I think you should get some ice on it as soon as possible. If you just tell me what you were planning to do, I'll finish the job while you go in and get that ice.

"Really, you don't have to do that. It can wait until later. The shutter blew loose in the last rainstorm, and I was nailing it back into place."

"Looks like I better secure it before we have another storm," Peter said, scanning the sky for nonexistent clouds. He kicked at the ground and a cloud of dust rose.

I took a few steps toward the house and turned to watch Peter pick up the nails from the windowsill and start hammering. I was sure he knew the shutter had been loose a long time. How long had it been since someone took time to care about anything I cared about? My to-do list had long ago grown into a book.

Indoors, I struck my black and blue thumb into a tall glass of ice water. From the kitchen window, I watched Mr. Fix-It Man. His moves were quick, confident, with no wasted movements. Within minutes he appeared at the back screen door and opened it just enough to stick in his head inside.

"Your shutter is as good as new. While I was at it, I noticed the other shutter was missing a nail, so I replaced that one too." Quietness hung in the air like a class waiting for the teacher to speak. "Do you mind if I invite myself in?"

"I'm sorry, come on in, excuse my rudeness, please come in and sit down." With glass in hand, I moved to the kitchen table and sat down on the chair. Peter had pulled out for me. "How much do I owe you for your time?"

"Please! Don't insult me. Helping out is what neighbors do," he said, looking into my eyes. I quickly dropped my eyes to the glass of water in front of me. I could feel his eyes follow mine. "Can I take a look at that thumb?" he asked.

"It's beginning to feel better or maybe I've just lost all feeling from the ice."

Peter reached down and took hold of the chair between his legs and pulled his chair closer to mine.

"Really, it's okay," I said, trying hard to sound convincing. The scent of his after shave intoxicated me.

"I believe you're right, but I would be happy to take a look. Helping out, remember that's what neighbors do?" Peter spoke softly, lifting my hand out of the glass of water and dabbing it with the towel I'd left lying on the table. Carefully and gently, he moved my thumb first to the left and then to the right. "Does this hurt?" "Can you feel this?" I tried to focus on his questions, but all I could think about was how my hand felt in his. I took in the dark hair on the back of his hand forming little curls and his well-manicured nails. His fingers were strong and firm yet gentle and soft. "Finally, how about this?" he said while slowing beginning moving it in a circular motion.

The pain lifted me from my chair.

"Sorry about that... Emma, I think you're going to need an x-ray to make sure there are no broken bones and release the pressure building up behind your nail."

"How do you know so much about hands?"

"It's my business."

"Your business? Aren't you a carpenter? The way you work with a hammer, I assumed you were a carpenter."

Peter held my hand in both his hands, "My dad's the carpenter. I learned everything I know from him. I do woodworking to relax. It's a hobby."

"A hobby? What do you do when you are not woodworking?"

"I'm an orthopedic surgeon." Peter paused before adding, "My specialty is hands."

"You're a hand specialist?"

A sheepish smile played at the corners of his mouth, he nodded and shrugged his shoulders, "What's a guy to do? A man must make a living. And besides I enjoy holding hands with a pretty lady like you."

"Well, Doctor Warner, I can see I'm in good hands."

Terri DeGezelle Michels

Edward Wills is a writer living in Eastern North Carolina. Formerly, he was a reporter at three Midwestern newspapers, a magazine editor, and a non-profit executive.

Lovers' Leap

"I dare you. If you're not scared, you'll jump over the edge to the other side. My uncle did it last week," LaKisha challenged.

Kwame 's big, brown eyes stared straight ahead, as if he were weighing the decision. It was only eight feet to the other side of the rock ledge, but it was 26 feet to the bottom. He knew. The nearby plaque at Raccoon Lake State Park and he had read it. It warned--in big red letters-- against jumping to the other side. Young lovers considered the leap a test of true love.

They had for more than a century when William Simpson sought to prove his love for Mildred Washington. He almost made it. One foot landed on the other side before he slipped to an unpleasant death on the rocks below.

Since then, several young men made the leap. Most did. The few who didn't had their names carved into the giant oak tree, whose knotted branches spun skyward. But Kwame was afraid mostly to be chicken in front of LaKisha. Her long-black braids and brown skin was the stuff of his dreams. At 13, there stood his perfect women. But would a perfect woman ask you to risk your life on a dare?

He knew the small gathering of friends who stood by watching would spread the story throughout the school in no time. By the arrival of the yellow school bus back at Martin Luther King Middle School, most of the seventh grade would know. Thank you Facebook.

133

Kwame's brain sped like a freight train. He knew better than to attempt the leap. He knew too that LaKisha was lying about her uncle having made the leap. She didn't have an uncle. Only two aunts.

His eyes sparked with fear: Fear of seeming a coward before his perfect woman and of what his crushed body would look like sprawled on the rocks.

"Don't do it Kwame," Byron called from the group of onlooking friends. "She just wants the excitement of seeing you leap. She doesn't care if you get killed."

LaKisha stood with her hands in her pockets as if she didn't have a care in the world.

All of 12 years old, Kwame thought of his chances. If he got a running start, he could make it. Or could he?

What will you give me if I make it? Kwame asked.

"A kiss." came the temptress's reply. Kwame was desperate for a smooch. He followed her around looking for opportunities to impress her, like a puppy dog jumping up and down for attention.

Shy Kwame had never been kissed, except by his mom, a kiss from LaKisha, Wow. It was the stuff of dreams.

But death was forever. No one ever accused a 12-year-old boy of overthinking a situation. Maybe Kwame would be the first.

"Don't do it Kwame," screamed Lauren. "You don't have to prove anything." Lauren liked Kwame. He was her perfect man. She, too, was afraid to let Kwame know of her crush.

Getting ready to jump, Kwame backed up about 15 feet. For some reason, he crouched imitating an Olympic sprinter he had seen on television. No one said ready, set, go. No one fired a starter's pistol. His body just started to move. After five feet, he was upright and moving full speed

ahead on the narrow dirt path past the ever-present pine
trees. At 10 feet, the dress shoes on his feet slipped
revealing why runners did not wear them. At the edge, time
stood still. Or did it speed up? Kwame could not tell. He
raised his feet like a 747 taking off at the airport and hurled
himself into space.

How long is an eternity? How short is forever?
Every onlookers' eyes were on Kwame.

Mid way through the leap, wind flying through his
curly hair, his legs started coming down. But were they
landing on solid ground or solid air that would not support
his weight. Finally, his feet touched down on solid ground.
He made it with more than six inches to spare. A collective
sigh rose from his classmates, including LaKisha.

"I am not a coward," he screamed to no one in
particular. Followed by "I made it." Moving by themselves,
his feet broke into a jig. A broad smile stretched across his
face. All seemed right with the world.

When he looked back at the group, Lauren's face smiled.
Byron's grinned as he yelled "You did it Kwame." But Mrs.
Brown, who had returned from taking the sick child to the
bus, was angry. Her face snarled as if she'd bitten into a
lemon.
"Kwame Johnson of all the silly stunts I've seen in my 18
years of teaching, this is the dumbest. You could have killed
yourself. I'll bet you'll wish you had never done this when
your mother finds out what you did." We will meet you
back at the bus. And, the shrill in her voice rising, don't you
even think about jumping back over here. You'll have to take
that trail. Just start walking. It's only about two miles from
that side.

By the time Kwame got back, all eyes were on him.
They'd all seen what he did. He was an instant legend.

They'd tell their grandkids about the leap. Some would tell how stupid it was. Others how heroic. Still others how romantic.

But the leap had changed Kwame. In those eight seconds he'd found a new confidence. He'd added a hitch to his step. An eternal strut. He wasn't scared of anything anymore.

He saw LaKisha sitting alone at the back of the buses. Nearly as sure of himself as John Wayne, he started walking toward her. When he got there, not waiting for permission, he kissed her. On the mouth. Tongue too. The students cheered.

LaKisha didn't struggle. She willingly paid up for the bet. She kind of liked it. She hoped there would be more, but not today.

Mrs. Taylor grabbed him by his collar. She made him sit next to her for the ride home. Not even what his mother might do to him could take the smile from his face.

Edward Wills

Sarah Merritt Ryan is a published academic, a commercial blogger, and has poetry published in Hope Whispers, Whispering Angels Books. She is a Triangle, North Carolina native who has a lifelong passion for creative writing through poetry and creative nonfiction. Her creative spark is found through nature, people, and reflection.

Truth

My worst dreams came true
Realities struck a spectrum of blues
Penetrating deep into paralysis
A timeless, empty cocoon

I see and remember excuses that were
Like old friends, a victory in disguise
As lies one day will be uncovered
Enough for me to recognize

One day the truth will find me
Coaxing me to focus my salvaged parts
Lifting my soul from the depths of a deceptive oasis
To boldly reenter what I never understood

Alive

Breath comes in and rolls out
Quietness, stark clarity within
Holding onto shadows inside
Like a dark figment of history claimed

Searching for my soul exhausting
Never-ending circles endured
Finding meaning wanting
Love down deep secured

Wisps of a startling breeze
Like ice shooting up my spine
Truth hurts I know all too well
Alive enough for tears and fears

Is there enough life left
To smile with my eyes
To pray with my heart
While there is still time

Using my mind to pretend
Talking the talk
Nothing left inside
Running on fumes giving up

So weary my soul
Fighting for change
Wrestling with reality
To live anew

Fallen Blue

Tick tock, tick tock the clock tells me
Wake up, wake up the heart inside of me says
It's safe, safe to come out and be alive
To exist, to love, even with the chance of losing again

How deeper can blue be than so washed out
The glow could be so much more brilliant
Hide I so deep and repressed inside
The light within leaps but can't yet reach the outside

Must I feel and relive to live again
Must I dare to win and reclaim my life
Stifled, muffled feelings must be heard
Like it or not world, I must be free

So tormented, world-abused I'm blind
Blinded by naivety first and second by tears
No words can utter what has happened
No explanation or logic will succeed

Who knew how my life would unfold
How victory I would see with my own eyes
Eyes with a jaded, cool tone
Wanting to celebrate yet so weary

So lucky am I to see the light of day
Like the end of a never-ending battle
I'm here, I'm alive and that's what matters
But am I really here, or can I be?

Have I disappeared too soon?
Too weak of heart at this moment
To seize my life and charge forward
Or do I simply fall away and let go

A decision I must make
I know the right answer to take
I want to live but don't know how
I've just been through too much pain

I have so much to live for
All my wildest dreams have come true
So why can't a break through this fog of emotion
And claim what God has gifted me?

Sarah Merritt Ryan

Drew Becker is a multi-book author, poet, writing coach, branding architect, and publisher at Realization Press (RealizationPress.com). His recent book, The Joyful Brand: Personal Branding for Authors, Speakers and the Rest of Us, includes exercises to help define personal brands. He collaborates with authors to help them publish and prosper.

Small World

Returning home one evening, Paxton thought he heard a sound when he walked through the door.

"Who's there?" he asked, the question aimed at no one. After getting no response, he changed out of his work clothes to jeans and a T-shirt, picking the latter off a chair and tossing the former back onto it. Kicking his shoes off, he lay on his bed, his eyes closed. Rousing himself from almost drifting off, he meandered to the kitchen to cook macaroni and cheese and bake a pan of cinnamon rolls for dinner. Later, after he had read another chapter in his book and watched the news on TV, he fell into a shallow slumber.

Paxton had been forced to take a low-level job in what had been his family's business just months ago. His position was part of the settlement when his father stepped down from his position of owner and CEO of the company. His parents had disappeared shortly after signing the agreement when their car careened off the side of a mountain. The authorities never recovered their bodies from the fiery wreckage. So, at 25, Paxton inherited a job for life, their moderate savings and stocks, and ownership of their property.

The house, while not lavish, included some unique and hidden characteristics but did not speak of wealth, although it was more palatial and twice the size of the surrounding homes. Constructed on a spacious three-acre lot—treed and grassy—the contrasting beige-tinted dwelling provided a certain privacy. Neighbors considered it somewhat mysterious. Many of them envied the home and kept their distance either out of respect or a sense that the family considered themselves somehow superior. However, this was not the case; the family simply embraced reticence and, though they would greet their neighbors with a nod or a smile, none of them felt at ease around others.

Before the changes, as a privileged son, his duties were minimal; he only attended meetings and watched executives as they consulted with his father to make decisions.

"He is being groomed for the future and doesn't need to take on any more responsibility for now," his mother would say. "We considered greater freedom an advantage neither of us had, so this is one thing we can pass on to our son."

Paxton's life had been idyllic, and he basked in his fortunate circumstances. Unlike some other endowed acquaintances, he did not indulge himself and was not a social butterfly, a flashy dresser, or a braggart. He preferred books and solitude to clubbing and rowdy parties.

When asked about his son's relationships, his mother would explain, "After a spate of mildly successful dating, my son has become increasingly introverted, and I expect him to remain an unwitting bachelor. His minimalistic life with few friends, his reading and increasing solitude seems sufficient for him."

After his parents lost control of the company, Paxton threw himself into the mundane work. Their sudden disappearance and finding out that they had transferred assets to his name without his knowledge created a nebulous uncertainty. However, he somehow knew not to look for his parents, fantasizing that this was part of a secret plan they had not shared with him. Over months, he had emptied many of the rooms in their home of the most poignant reminders of his mother and father and had sunk into his own world.

"I think they might still be alive somewhere, starting a new and different life," he confided to his psychiatrist.

In spite of Paxton's cavalier external attitude, the doctor thought their accident and disappearance tormented him and his denial retarded his recovery.

Paxton was coping and had settled into a necessary routine. Although the work was unchallenging, it tired him, perhaps because it was so banal. Night after night, he arrived home exhausted, wanting only to read or watch television before retiring. He refused to admit that these unfortunate events distracted him from basic tasks, including housekeeping. Towering plates topped with pots and pans usually erupted from the sink, reminding him of Jenga. He rarely dusted and would forget to put papers and mail away. He'd attend to the chaos on the weekends, cleaning up just enough to trudge into the following week.

Since losing his parents, something unexplainable kept occurring. He was slow to notice that small portions of food continued to disappear from his fridge and shelves. First, a chunk of cheddar cheese and a quarter loaf of multi-grained bread, then a few fruit cups, occasional bottles of water from a 12-pack, mini packages of raisins, a glass container of lemonade—not all at once but scattered over the month. He thought he might have been his own secret nighttime fridge raider while sleepwalking or mistakenly believed that he had purchased items he hadn't.

These episodes occurred infrequently enough that he ignored them. Maybe it was mice, he told himself, but purchased a handgun for protection anyway. He had no desire to focus on these disappearances, so he let them go, expecting to make time over the next weekend to investigate. When he got busy dealing with the chaos from the previous week, he forgot to follow up.

One night, during his restless sleep, a noise from the closet awakened him. He imagined it might be one of those mice or another outdoor creature that had invaded the house while he was at work. Considering it might be the culprit stealing his food, Paxton flung open the closet door, expecting to spot some kind of thief, but only saw his clothes and the brown-tinted storage boxes on the shelf above. Nothing seemed out of place. He returned to his bed.

The next day he talked to a coworker about it. "I could have sworn I heard something rummaging in my closet last night, but when I looked, there wasn't anything I could see. I checked again this morning, but everything is still in place."

"Maybe it was your—" his coworker began, but stopped short, realizing it would be a faux pas to suggest his missing parents. "Maybe it was your imagination or maybe you were dreaming. Or maybe this will develop into an auspicious event."

"A what?"

"Never mind."

This brief conversation reignited his curiosity, and he was determined to figure out what was going on. So, when he arrived home that evening, he went to the closet and pulled back the clothes. Behind them, he saw three discernable edges in the back wall and remembered from his childhood that there was a barely visible, secret entrance to a hiding place there. He recalled concealing himself there when he didn't want to be found. Only with age did he realize that his parents merely pretended not to find him. Only with age had he forgotten about his sanctuary.

Holding the handgun, he pushed with his other hand on the drywall and stooped to enter the secret hallway. Looking around, he didn't see anything, so he stepped backward into his bedroom, then resumed his ritual of television but skipped dinner and, exhausted, dropped onto his bed early. After tossing and turning for what seemed like hours but was only 20 minutes, he fell asleep, still contemplating the hidden passageway.

When he awakened to another sound from the closet, the room was dim, but still held onto the last vestiges of evening light. He tiptoed to the drawer and withdrew his gun again. He crept to the door and, swinging it open, holding the gun in the other hand, Paxton stood face to face with a frail figure.

"Yeee!" her voice squealed, and she bolted back with her arms raised in the air. Shaking, she stood there, her gaunt, pale skin shining like porcelain against her jet-black hair. Her head tilted downward so he couldn't see her face or eyes, only her slumped shoulders and bowed head. She looked up cautiously. He confronted a young lady whose face was slightly familiar.

"Who are you, and why are you here in my closet?"

A timid voice replied, "You probably don't remember me. My name doesn't matter. My whole world has shrunk into this tiny space. I have discovered a world behind this wall. I have set up a mattress, a table, a chair, and a few of my other things here."

He interrupted her. "You do remind me of someone, but I can't place you. What's your name? In spite of what you say, it does matter."

"Mizuki, Mizuki Ashen," she answered softly.

145

"Tell me, though, why would you limit yourself to live behind my closet? I know there is some space back there, but why would you want to hide in there?"

"It's a sad story. Six months ago, my family was evicted from our house. My parents went to live with my sister, but I didn't go."

"Okay, but how did you end up here—in my closet? And how did you even know it was here?"

"As a child, when you helped your father move your stuff into this large house with your inviting red front door, I watched from across the street. From my second-story bedroom window, I could see through your window on the third story. I peered between the branches of the sweetgums and the pines. I knew you had no brothers or sisters and wondered about your mother. My family and in fact the whole neighborhood was afraid of this house. There was a rumor that people had gone missing from this place over the last 40 years since it was built. We all called it 'the monster house.' Our parents prohibited us from saying anything about it, especially to you and your family. My family was very superstitious when I grew up. They warned me to stay away from anyone who lived here. My mother also believed that social standing selects the people you spend time with.

"Day after day, from behind the semi-sheer curtains, I looked at your window and fantasized. How could I sneak across the street to meet you? It seemed impossible. Your family stayed isolated from the rest of us, and they sent you to a school somewhere else. As I got older, plans for a secret meeting filled my mind."

"Yes," he replied. "They spent much of our wealth on their new business and to send me to a private school. But I remember, on occasion, seeing a phantom face staring from a small window in the house across the street."

"One day during the summer when my family had left me alone, I sneaked across the street, and you must have seen me coming because you met me on the front lawn, and we retreated behind the garden. I was so happy. We met just two more times, and I loved talking to you. That's when you told me about your secret closet.

"Tearful, at 14, I watched as you left for school. We hadn't seen each other for months, and I didn't even consider that you would go away to college. I cursed myself for never contacting you.

"Weeks later, my mother asked me, 'Why so sullen?' She knew nothing of my dreams.

"'He's gone, and you stopped me from meeting him. I will never have the chance to follow the golden road that could have been,' I blurted out.

"'Who are you talking about?' she asked, taken aback by my forcefulness.

"'The boy across the street. He was to be my chance,' I answered. 'But, no, you and father decided we do not mingle with dragon-red door people, that we do not talk with those of a higher station. My chance is gone forever.'

"'Daughter, do not fret. No melodrama. You are still young and will meet others who have more in common with you,' she replied, trying to reassure me. 'You cannot force life to your mold; let it unfold instead and you will be much happier.'"

As soon as Mizuki stopped talking, Paxton invited her into the house proper. "Come into the kitchen. Let me fix you something to eat. So how have you survived? I know groceries have gone missing, but I wouldn't have thought it was enough to sustain someone."

She sheepishly peered down at the plate he had filled with a well-fried omelet. He sat down across from her after sliding a portion onto his plate.

She turned her gaze toward the breakfast he had prepared for them.

"But I could not get you out of my mind. Even as I entered high school, I remained alone. My girlfriends found boyfriends. The other girls told me I had beautiful hair and eyes, and, as my body matured, they said I had a haunting presence. But I had no interest in anyone's advances. I was stuck in time, thinking of the boy who had lived in the house with the dragon-red door."

Now he lowered his head to hide the scarlet that raced across his face. He reached out to raise her head but withdrew his hand and asked, "How did you come to live in my closet?"

"I only discovered your name and that your family had once been extremely rich before… you know, before your family lost the company. After searching for years, I saw you on the street. I followed you back to this house. You were carrying a couple of bags of groceries. I slipped in behind you and found your closet as you were bringing in more. I made myself comfortable. After you would leave for work, I'd go to the fridge or cupboard to get small portions of food, then retreat before you'd get back. I've watched you from the closet every evening and then hid behind boxes in the morning when you got your clothes."

"There's more to the story, right?" Paxton asked.

"Yes, but…"

He could not control himself any longer and, grasping her chin, elevated her face. He saw her crystal-blue eyes and lips down-turned at the edges. In her eyes, he saw a reflection of gold and silver from the lights in the room. A smile blossomed on his lips.

"Now I remember. We did talk a few times; we met out behind the garden. I couldn't understand how you could walk barefoot over those sweetgum sticker balls. Because you were always so nervous, I was too timid to ask."

"I certainly remember you, Mizuki Ashen. You are welcome to stay, but we will have to move you to one of the empty bedrooms. We can share the house and, to tell you the truth, I have been feeling like I need the company. Let's see where this goes." He suppressed the delight that tried to creep up into his face.

She bowed and thanked him. Her face also gave over to a shy smile. She whispered, "Your mother and father say hello."

Drew Becker

Ana Shapkaliska is a scriptwriter, novelist, and short story writer from North Macedonia. Many of her TV projects in Europe won awards at European TV Festivals. Her novel "Govinda, Anuttam and the Juhu Temple" was published by TRI. She lives with her husband in Cary, North Carolina. www.anashapkaliska.com

Hope Avenue
(Dedicated to Lalitha)

Just as Frosina thought how boring that Saturday afternoon was, that nothing exciting was going on in her life, the house phone started to ring. It was her husband Govind's ex-wife, calling to ask about him. Frosina politely replied that he was taking rest and she would convey the message as soon as he was up.

Her husband's ex called every day, always with the same question: "How is Govind coming along with getting a professional job? Is he trying hard enough?"

Frosina and Govind responded patiently and with kindness: "As soon as there's good news, you'll be the first one to know about it. We are doing our best."

Frosina's brief stay in the United States confirmed what her father-in-law had told her about his ex, but Frosina was sometimes surprisingly naive, refusing to believe. She was one of those people who liked to experience things on her own. She wanted to be unbiased and open at heart in her dealings with others. She even hoped she could become best friends with the ex. That was her sincere desire. So, whenever some of her girlfriends would laugh in her face and tell her, "You're crazy. Judging by the way she treats you both, she must be a very envious and jealous person,"

150

Frosina couldn't accept it. She thought, given enough love, anyone's heart could melt.

And when her father-in-law talked about the ex that she is a mean person, Frosina thought, 'When people divorce, the other side is always the villain,' so she didn't take his words at face value. But lately there had been plenty of opportunities to experience that malice on her own skin. The ex used to call every single day, sometimes even twice a day, and harass Govind about not getting a job in his field, and being a taxi driver. Frosina somehow managed to tolerate the insults directed towards her, but whenever the ex started vilifying her husband, she would politely end the conversation.

Today was the same story. After hanging up the phone, she sighed deeply.

"Lord, what have I done so wrong that You are putting me in these situations, to deal with people who don't hesitate to make my life miserable, over and over again?"

She tried to forget about the ex and even sent her a blessing in her heart. "I should pray more for this person," she thought.

Within less than five minutes, the phone rang again.

"Oh no," Frosina thought. "If it's his ex again, I don't know if I'll have the strength to be so polite." She hesitated to pick up the phone, but the thought that the ringing might wake up her husband prompted her to answer. With a deep sigh, the unpleasant conversation still ringing in her head, she answered, "Hello."

"Hello, Frosina." It was the familiar voice of her good friend Shalini.

"Hi, Shalini. How are you?"

"Mmm, the news I have is not that good."

"Why, what happened?"

"Remember Anusha?"

"Anusha? That beautiful little girl who played the flute during the Sunday Feast at the temple?"

"Yes."

"What about her?"

"She died in a car accident. Some African guy ran her over with his SUV."

**

Anusha's family lived in a large and beautiful home on Ruthwin Dr. in Morrisville, North Carolina, an upper middle-class neighborhood. It took Frosina and Govind twenty-five minutes to drive from Cary to get to the memorial organized to honor Anusha. The entire street was full of cars parked on both sides. There were hundreds of pairs of shoes in front of the entrance.

The night before, Frosina couldn't sleep at all, thinking about Anusha and her sudden death. Analyses and assumptions failed to put her heart at ease; they made her even more restless. She tried to read herself to sleep with 'Midaq Alley' by Nagib Mahfouz, but to no avail. The thought of Anusha being no more caused her a lot of pain. She felt such grief for the beautiful twelve-year-old, even though she had only seen her twice.

At the ISKCON temple in Hillsborough, a sumptuous vegetarian feast was served after every Sunday program. When Frosina visited the temple for the first time, it so happened that she sat next to Anusha at the dinner table. She thought, "How fortunate is this little girl . . . Born into a brahminical family, knowing about Krishna ever since she was born." Then just a week before the accident, she saw her for the second and last time. Anusha played the flute at the Sunday program. Frosina remembered with sadness in her

152

heart how loudly she had applauded after the performance, to encourage the girl. She didn't just like her playing; she was captivated by the girl's graceful features.

"This girl is special. It's as if she doesn't belong to this world. Some special star enlightens her way," she thought.

And then, the very next day, Anusha was no longer there.

"Only after someone dies do we remember how fragile we are, like an egg falling to the floor and shattering into so many pieces." Frosina remembered these words her grandmother, Draga, used to say.

The fairly large living room was filled to capacity with the devotees from the Hillsborough temple, the larger part of the local congregation, and the closest friends of Anusha's family. Everyone was sitting cross-legged on the floor. Despite the size of the crowd, the air in the room was not stifling. The windows were wide open. It was a beautiful spring morning with the fragrances of blossoming trees all around. Birds chirped joyfully, and squirrels frolicked in the grass and trees.

Frosina sat down towards the back, on the side with the women, and Govind mingled with the men. The atmosphere was heavy and solemn. There was whispering in the room among some of the guests, and sorrow in everyone's eyes. The spirit of death hung over everyone in all its gloom.

Frosina sat next to Savitri, a transgender who was a member of the congregation. At Frosina's first visit to the temple, Savitri had immediately caught her eye. The very same evening, upon returning home, she asked Govind, "Who is that lady? She's the most beautiful woman in the temple."

Govind hesitated at first, but then he told her, in brief, the story of how the man Satsvarup was now living as Savitri.

Frosina never despised her for that, unlike many, who laughed behind her back. She made friends with her and occasionally invited Savitri to her home.

"I'm so sorry about Anusha," said Frosina.

"It's not easy, but everything is in God's hands, and we don't know why this was supposed to happen," Savitri replied.

Frosina's husband was a favorite singer among the devotees. He had a wonderful voice and was called to lead the bhajans whenever he was amongst the devotees. This day was no different. When Govind's voice spread around the room, it lifted the heaviness and melted the leaden feeling in the hearts of the devotees. They followed his lead in singing, and the atmosphere became transcendental.

Frosina sang with her eyes closed. The words of the song melted her heart:

"Why do you worry when Radha and Krishna are always with you... Always with you...
And the wise man knows the soul has no death... We all have a mission on Earth,
And Krishna knows when it's time to leave..."

There was a wonderful altar in the room, with many Deities—Sri Sri Radha-Syamasundar, Sri Sri Gaura-Nitai, Sri Lakshmi-Narasimha, Shiva, and Ganesh—all decorated with garlands of fresh flowers that Anusha's mother Lalitha, had made that morning. In the middle, there was a picture of Anusha's smiling face.

Sitting near the altar, weeping softly, Lalitha wiped her tears with a white handkerchief. She was extremely beautiful; she looked like one of those famous Indian supermodels.

154

"It must be so hard on her," thought Frosina. "It was only two days ago that her daughter's body was cremated."

Govind began a new bhajan and the devotees followed. Frosina turned towards Savitri and saw her face all in tears. She gently squeezed her arm. Savitri started crying even more profusely.

At the conclusion of the bhajans, Govind put the mridanga against the wall, and stood there beside Anusha's father, Vasudev.

Krishna Lila, an elderly nun amongst the congregation, was invited to deliver the eulogy. She was well known for her devotion and virtue, and many considered her to be a pure devotee of the Lord.

"Everything in this material world has its end, except the love God has for us. That love is forever. God never leaves us; He is always with us. It is not so easy accepting the change that Anusha is no longer among us, but I'm sure she is in a much better place now than we are. God in my heart is telling me this. The greatest gift in this world is to be born in a family of dedicated devotees. Anusha had this good fortune. From her very birth, she was guided on the path to love and understand God, and what she achieved during her brief stay on Earth is not accomplished by many, even after several lifetimes. People who are loved, never die."

Lalitha took a garland from the altar and gave it to Krishna Lila, then invited all the guests to help themselves to prasadam . The house was quite large, but with so many guests, it was hard to walk around. Frosina had no appetite and could not understand how anyone could eat at all. Sneaking into the hallway, she saw Anusha's pictures pinned to two large Styrofoam boards, together with the things that she had liked and done in her brief life. Frosina stood transfixed before the boards, eager to satisfy her curiosity.

Even as a little girl, she had been curious about the phenomenon of death. When she was three years old, she realized she didn't want to die and yet wouldn't be able to avoid it, and was constantly wondering: "Why was I born? Why must I die? And where do we go after death?"

She read from the first board:

Memories of Anusha's past as she lived it:

These are some of my favorite things:

Activity: Riding a bike when it's raining

Dress: Saree

Instrument: Flute

Movie: Pirates of the Caribbean

Indian series: Mahabharata

Food: Rasam and Okra

Comfort food: Macaroni and cheese

Fruit: Mango

Color: Pink-blue-lime green

Role models: Maternal grandmother and Mother Theresa

Indian movie: Lagaan

Anusha's last memorable moments:

Movie: Meet the Robinsons

Concert: New Goloka dham, ISKCON Temple, Hillsborough, NC

Birthday party: Samhita's

Trip: India

Words to Mommy: Good night

Greeting "Ram, Ram"

Project: Science-DNA

Library books: 50 years of DNA, Genetics demystified

Web site: Gandhiji's quotes

Quotes discussed with family:

"I believe in equality for everyone, expect reporters &
photographers."

"I do not want to foresee the future. I'm concerned with
taking care of the present. God has given me no control over
the moment following." Mahatma Gandhi

Celebration Occasion: NC State Recognition for 7th
Grade SAT Score. Parents treat at "Sweet Tomatoes".
My choice of celebration: To spend time at "Barnes &
Noble" ("Something we have in common," Frosina thought.)

Book: Morning is Long Time Coming – Bette Green

Anusha's poem written about Lord Krishna:

Although I have forgotten You

For so many long years,

In this material world,

Today, I'm surrendering unto You.

I'm Your sincere and serious servant.

Please engage me in Your service,

My dear Lord,

From this day, I'm Yours, Anusha.

On the second board, there were many photographs showing
Anusha in all kinds of outfits. She had played roles in many
plays, depicting the powerful characters such as Yashoda,
Gopi, Radharani, Draupadi, Rukmini, Vishakha, all from the
Indian culture and religion.

Also pinned here was the fifth-grade certificate: Fifth
Grade Celebration:

This is to certify that Anusha Vasudeva has satisfactorily
completed the course of study prescribed for the William H.
Fuller G. T. Magnate Elementary School, and is therefore
entitled to this certificate given at Raleigh, NC, this 25th of
May 2005... Principal, Brandon Johns... Teacher, Molly
Smith... Assistant Principal, Ann Jackson...

157

There were many pictures with Anusha in all kinds of places—at a restaurant, at school, her mom's workplace, birthday parties, in front of the new house, the old house, in India...

Frosina always carried a notebook in her purse, and while the others were eating, she stealthily wrote down everything she could see on the boards. Someone approached her from behind. She turned around. It was Lalitha.

"Why don't you take prasadam? Aren't you hungry?"

"I'll have some later," Frosina lied. She knew it wasn't polite to refuse prasadam.

"What are you writing?" Lalitha asked curiously, without a trace of reproach.

Frosina hesitated to tell her, but then she lifted her face and looked straight into Lalitha's eyes.

"I wrote down everything that was on these two boards. I want to write a story about Anusha, but I'd never do that without your blessing."

Lalitha looked at her silently with a gentle expression.

"Do you know how much Anusha loved music?"

Frosina nodded.

"Come, I'll show you something that might help you for your story."

Lalitha went upstairs with Frosina in tow. They stopped at a door. "This is Anusha's room," she said.

She opened it. Among other things, one that immediately caught Frosina's attention was a yellow board that had written on it with a black marker:

My current goals (Anusha Vasudeva)

I, Anusha, being of "sound" mind, body & spirit, do resolve to do the following things to make music a more important part of my life:

Buy & practice more music; organize all the flute music that I have; practice at least thirty minutes to one hour per day; try to conduct & compose my own music; use my tuner more often; I would like to learn bass clef; to become a little more serious about playing the piccolo; I want to make sure I record music right after I play it; I want to clean my flute more often…

"It's not how good we are, but what good things we do…" Anusha Vasudeva

Star student: To ANUSHA VASUDEVA, for receiving all A's this year, Congratulations, From Mrs. Tillery…

"Can I write all this down?"

Lalitha nodded, "Go ahead," and left the room.

Frosina got chills all over.

"Oh my God, just days ago, Anusha studied and slept in this room, greeted her friends, ate and laughed, talked on the phone, did her homework and played on the computer, listened to music and played the flute. And now, all that is here is the urn with her ashes."

She thought of going downstairs and joining the devotees. Her husband would certainly be wondering where she had disappeared. Just as she started to leave, her attention was captured by a pink sheet of paper on the wall next to the window.

A POEM FOR MY SISTER VAISHNAVI, ANUSHA VASUDEVA

TITLE: BLACK BEADY EYES

"When I first looked at her, her eyes were closed, my Joy
knew no bounds!
When she first looked at me, I couldn't stop smiling with
glee!
When she first smiled at me, my feeling came up to say,
She is growing up, Hooray.
When she first rolled over, I screamed like a red rover.
When I watched her sprout and see her future milestones, I'll
be proud within!
And most of all I'm really happy, when my baby sister looks
at me,
With her black beady eyes, and receive a smile every single
time."

**

In the funeral parlor two days ago, Frosina sat in the front
row. She listened to the eulogies very carefully delivered by
Anusha's school friends, teachers, the principal, her
relatives, and friends of the family. All of them spoke about
how special and wonderful Anusha was, and how they
would never forget her. Frosina was trying hard to figure out
some signs, something mystical in what she had heard,
something that would shed some light on why Anusha had to
die—but nothing, not a single clue. The little girl's death
was still a great enigma for her.

Lying on the white satin insides of the coffin, Anusha
was like a gorgeous sleeping doll. Frosina even thought that
she wore make-up. Her eyelashes looked unusually long and
thick, and her cheeks were not pale either.

Her maternal grandparents were sitting beside the coffin,
grandfather at her head and grandmother at her feet. They

were sitting straight, looking dignified, but their eyes had a
lifeless look.

After the eulogies, two Indian priests chanted mantras, and at
the end of the ritual, invited everyone present to repeat after
them the names of Krishna and Govinda.

Anusha's father stood by the coffin, looking at his
daughter with indescribable love and pain. "If God only saw
the look in his eyes, He would certainly bring her back to
life," Frosina thought. But then she remembered that God
knows everything, and Frosina felt puzzled again about the
mystery why Anusha had to die.

"Why is He breaking the hearts of these good people?"
They are beautiful, intelligent, educated, religious. Both
from brahminical families, both with Master's degrees in IT.
Both from South India by origin. Lalitha worked for IBM,
and Vasudev for Cisco Systems.

After the whole funeral ceremony was over, Lalitha and
Vasudev thanked all the guests and announced that the final
part (going to the crematorium) was private, open only to the
closest family members and the priests. Frosina was eager to
go too, and begged Govind to ask Lalitha and Vasudev if
they could come as well. Govind was determined to ask, but
in the commotion created as everyone was leaving, they
were late getting outside and the cars heading to the
cremating spot had already disappeared down the lane.
Frosina and Govind stood there watching people leave, and
she thought her last chance of unraveling the mystery to
Anusha's death had been lost.

She had, in a way, expected a miracle, a voice from
heaven, from God Himself to tell her why He had to arrange
it that way, to tell her where Anusha was now and what she
was doing at the moment. She firmly believed that God

would actually speak to her in person, tap her on the shoulder and tell her the whole story. She had a burning desire to understand why Anusha had to leave. That was on Thursday.

**

And on Saturday, after she had written down the things that she planned to use for her story from Anusha's room, she went downstairs. The memorial was over and most of the guests had left. Lalitha and Vasudev stood in the hall talking to some of the remaining guests. Frosina joined in and found out from the conversation how the accident had taken place.

On April 9, 2007, her father drove her to school. Before Anusha walked out of the car, he hugged her and wished her a nice day. She walked out in front of the car with the intention of crossing the street to school. Just as she stepped out, a vehicle with great speed knocked her to the ground. The driver was some African guy, and it turned out that he was even staying illegally in the United States. He told the police that Anusha had run in front of his SUV at the last moment, and that there was nothing he could have done to avoid the accident.

But the truth was entirely different. Anusha was not running. On the contrary, he'd been speeding in a school zone.

Anusha's younger sister, Vaishnavi, came out of the living room. She was four. She raised her arms to her father and he picked her up. She whispered something into his ear, and they left the hallway.

"The hardest thing for them will be to explain to Vaishnavi where Anusha went," said Govind.

"Yes," said Frosina pensively. "Vaishnavi is so cute, so much like her sister in the face."

Someone asked Lalitha about what had happened to the driver that hit Anusha.

"He's free," Lalitha replied bitterly. "If I had been there, he wouldn't have gotten away so easily... Certainly, he feels bad too, having terrible sleepless nights, but what is his pain compared to ours?"

Frosina was perplexed about how someone that ran over and killed a person was not immediately sent to prison, as was the case in her own country. There was no pardoning such people, even though it was an accident, they had to do at least some time in jail.

Frosina also found out from the conversation that Anusha was born on December 2, 1994, and that she had started a charitable organization called 'Hope Avenue'. She wrote down the website address and could not wait to get home to check it out.

**

Excited, she sat down at the computer. "Can you believe," she said to Govind, "In just two and a half years, they managed to collect 150,000 dollars."

According to Lalitha, the two things that had profoundly touched Anusha were 9/11 and the Indonesian tsunami of 2004. She had cried bitterly in front of the TV when she saw those events, and started asking her parents, "How can we help these people? What can we do?" This way the organization called 'Hope Avenue' was founded in 2004 with headquarters in Raleigh. Anusha was barely ten years old at the time.

Helped by her parents, she organized mass production and distribution of cookies and pastries through all the larger food chains in the country. They themselves were surprised by the success, as if God Himself had inspired shoppers to

163

buy from 'Hope Avenue' without them even knowing that all the money went to charity.

Apart from that, Anusha had organized the distribution of drawings, greeting cards, calendars and ceramic ornaments made by elementary and high school kids, which also turned out to be an incredible success. Several times, she appeared on major TV stations news and in newspapers and magazines. Everyone was amazed when they discovered the age of the organization's founder and CEO. Frosina found some editions of 'The News & Observer': "In two and a half years, by the drive and hard work of Anusha Vasudeva, 'Hope Avenue' collected 150,000 dollars. Most of it was sent to the victims of the Indonesia tsunami, and the rest went to children with special needs in North Carolina."
"Wow," Frosina thought. "Unbelievable."

Lalitha and Vasudev had always been Anusha's greatest supporters. They always told her: "Don't stop dreaming! Don't stop creating wonderful things! In the summer, when you don't have school, we will back you up. Just keep on having new ideas."
She herself picked 'Hope Avenue' as the name of the charity. She never even thought about putting her own name on it.

**

"Dearest Anusha, I will always love you. I will never forget you. In my heart, there will always be a very special place for you…"
"Anusha, you have been a great inspiration for everybody around you – to the old and to the young. With your

example, you have shown us the path that we should follow…'

"One of the most talented and most wonderful students that I have ever had in my career…"

"Anusha, your wonderful music and spirit of kindness will lighten our way. I hope you are very happy in heaven…"

"Dearest Anusha, I had always admired you that you could ride a bike so much faster than me. You were my great role model because of that…"

Frosina kept reading through the notebook containing memories and impressions of Anusha. It's been over two years now since her death. She had almost finished the story about her, yet some details were missing. It had been a while since her death, the pain had subsided a bit, and on meeting Lalitha at the temple she asked her if they could talk about Anusha. She explained that she had been having trouble finishing the story. "I will be happy to help you," Lalitha immediately agreed.

She was in the seventh month of pregnancy. "I'm so happy for Lalitha... she's so glowing and gorgeous in her pregnancy," Frosina thought, temporarily forgetting her own pain over not being able to conceive.

As was prearranged, Govind took Frosina that evening to the house of Lalitha and Vasudev, and went off to drive his taxi for the night shift. Frosina came with gifts for everyone – Lalitha, Vasudev and Vaishnavi.

Upon entering the house, she found Lalitha sitting at a large table, working with several little girls on some new 'Hope Avenue' projects. They were designing bookmarks for distribution in North Carolina bookstores.

Frosina sat down with them. Each of the girls had drawn a few ideas and together with Lalitha, they were trying to pick the best ones. Soon, the girls left and Lalitha and Frosina went up to Anusha's room. Everything was exactly the same as it was two years ago, except the urn with the ashes was missing.

Lalitha started talking: "To declare someone dead, they wait for 24 hours. Even when they know right from the start that there is no hope, still, they don't declare them dead at once... The hardest part was explaining to Vaishnavi. She kept asking: 'Where is Anusha? Where is she? Why is she not here with me?' I would tell her that she is now with Krishna, but that would not satisfy Vaishnavi. She would start crying: 'Show me where she is! I want to see her face; I miss her so much...' Those were the most painful moments for us... And Vaishnavi went on with her questions: 'Why did she leave us and go to Krishna?' I said, 'Because she is happy being with Him'...Then she would ask me: 'Happier than being with us? I don't believe you! Tell me where she is. I want my tickle monster back...Promise me, that one day she will come back to us...Some evenings, if you and Daddy are not here, who is going to help me to brush my teeth? Who is going to help me to wear my pajamas?'... And she would start crying heavily again..."

Frosina knew that Indians were very respectful of astrology, and that they consulted an astrologer for every important event in their lives. When Lalitha and Vasudev decided to get married, they went to an astrologer to check their compatibility. When children are born, the parents immediately get their charts done to get at least some glimpse into their destiny.

"How come no astrologer warned you that such a thing would happen to Anusha?" Frosina asked, puzzled.

"Vasudev's father is quite a good astrologer, and a year and a half before she died, he actually did see death in her horoscope, but it was hard for him to accept it. And he didn't tell anyone. Only after her death, he revealed to us that he had seen that she wouldn't be with us for much longer."

"I see," Frosina said. "Such a thing is not easy to say, especially to your loved ones... And did you sense anything?"

"Yes. Six months before she died, I felt very strange. I was upset; I felt something terrible was going to happen. But I thought I was the one who would die. I felt a change coming, and that too, for the worse. But I didn't talk to anyone about it either, not even to Vasudev... He noticed that I was going through something, he even asked me a few times, but I didn't have the courage or the desire to discuss it... Yes, I definitely felt something. But if I may say so, Anusha's death brought a sensation previously unknown to me, and that is, I stopped fearing death. It is only natural that everyone is afraid of it, but I'm no longer afraid of death... The sweetest person in my life is gone, and I don't fear death anymore..."

"To you, what are the two most important things about Anusha?"

"The first is her deep spirituality. Anusha was truly religious. She always believed in Krishna, that He is the Supreme God. And whenever she was upset or confused, sad or angry, she wrote notes to Krishna. And the second thing about her is her generosity. She felt as though she had some mission in this world. Everyone in the family was amazed, how profound that feeling was in her, a girl so young... She knew the Mahabharata and Ramayana almost by heart – all the names, events, characters... Whenever someone asked her a question about those great epics, she would immediately give a perfect answer..."

"When she lay in the coffin at the funeral, was she wearing make-up?" Frosina felt a slight shiver from her directness in asking the questions.

"No, there was no make-up. I just wiped her face with a wet napkin. And we donated her internal organs – the heart, lungs and kidneys... When she saw a heart on her father's driving license (an organ donor in case of death), she immediately said: 'I will have a heart on my driving license too.'"

Lalitha sighed.

"Please tell me if this is too intense for you," Frosina was truly concerned.

"No. Because I love talking about Anusha. And I always will... Because to me, she is not dead and never will be... And very often she comes to me in my dreams, and to Vaishnavi too... It was only yesterday that Vaishnavi had a dream of them together on a playground, and Anusha hugged and kissed her... Anusha could not tolerate tears in my eyes, even if it was only from cutting onions. She would come and gently wipe them away... She was very connected to my mother too. They were so close. Anusha would tell her everything. She would confide about everything in her first, and then to Krishna. My mother is very devoted to God, and Anusha's death was such a shock to her. She wondered just like me: "What did I do so wrong, that I lost Anusha?"

"Anusha always followed ekadashi , and sometimes she would try a complete fast... She was happy about every trip to India, and we tried to make it there at least once a year... Vasudev and I come from brahminical families – Madhva sampradaya , and we regularly visited the Udupi temple. The last time we went with Anusha was during the summer of 2006. We visited the holy places Vrindavan, Mathura, Mayapur..."

"Kids usually like animals. Did Anusha like having pets?"

"Oh yes…She loved pets, animals. We were ready to fulfill that desire of hers too."

Frosina's eyes fell on the chest of drawers where Anusha's flute was sitting.

Lalitha noticed that and said: "'This is it, the right thing for me', Anusha would say. The flute was her favorite instrument."

"In this country, children can be a little racist," said Frosina. "Did Anusha ever feel despised by others just because she had a darker skin complexion?"

"I'm sure she wasn't that timid herself. Rather, she was very proud of her Indian heritage. And whenever some kid would taunt her about being Indian, she would very intelligently cut him down. She was as proud as a peacock, and would sometimes say: 'Maybe I was a peacock in my previous life.' When she died, she was in the seventh grade, although she was only twelve. She was a year ahead in her schooling."

"Where did you scatter her ashes?"

"Into the Kaveri. That is a holy river in South India."

Getting up from the floor, Lalitha opened a drawer, took out a magazine and handed it to Frosina. Anusha was on the front page.

"Without knowing that she is not alive anymore, they put her on the front page of this magazine (Indian Dance) …It was proclaimed the best photograph of the year."

Lalitha put the magazine back. "If you don't mind, let's go downstairs. In my condition, I have to eat something..."

"Sure." Frosina got up from the floor where she had been sitting cross-legged like her host, and they went down to the dining room.

Vasudev and Vaishnavi were out visiting the neighbors. Lalitha served two plates.

"Don't serve too much for me, please. I'll just have some fruits," Frosina asked.

"Okay."

"Thanks for setting aside some time for me... for telling me all these things."

"You are most welcome... I'll never stop talking about Anusha. Never... The day before she died was Sunday, April 8, 2007. That morning, she had finished all her homework, and she played with her friends, and in the afternoon, she watched Mahabharata. Suddenly it started to rain. She was really a girl who enjoyed biking in the rain. When the rain would start, she would take her bike and circle a few blocks around the neighborhood...We used to joke with Vasudev: 'Isn't she crazy? Like someone else I know'...That Tuesday, April 10, I fed Vaishnavi breakfast... I had just returned from the hospital where I kept an all-night vigil beside Anusha's bed together with Vasudev... I was rushing to get back to the hospital... Vaishnavi was eating cereal, and between mouthfuls, she said: 'I dreamt of Anusha playing basketball with Krishna.' My blood froze.

Anusha never liked basketball. Still, I managed to keep myself together in front of Vaishnavi, and calmly asked her: 'Is she happy playing? Is she playing well?'...Vaishnavi replied: 'No. She is not happy...And she is coughing.' I got back to the hospital as fast as I could... I sat with Vasudev by Anusha's bed. She had a million devices plugged into her body. We sat in silence. At 6:30 in the evening, the doctors came into the room, shut down the life support devices, and officially declared her dead. We sat on the bed, immovable, not even looking an inch away from Anusha. Only then it struck me how deeply attached I was to her... But I still

170

managed to say to her, 'You go baby... Go... I'm not keeping you here anymore... Just go... I love you most in the whole world, but I'm letting you go...'

Ana Shapkaliska

Nancy Lee Badger retired from her satisfying job as a 911 Emergency Medical Dispatcher. She is a member of Romance Writers of America, Heart of Carolina Romance Writers, Fantasy-Futuristic & Paranormal Romance Writers, and Triangle Association of Freelancers. She lives in Raleigh, North Carolina where she finds story ideas in the most unusual places.

A Rose from Richard

White petals
      folding lightly,
leafy fingers
      grasping tightly,
sweet perfumes
      gently swirling,
velvet crown
      humbly curling,
stems bending
      bowing lowly,
seedling grown
      dying slowly,
words unwritten
      feelings growing,
warmest wishes
      spread unknowing,
true emotions
      I tried resisting,
giving way to
      dreams existing.

Lessons from My Cat…the Dog

When my sister, a veterinarian, asked me to foster an orphaned orange tabby kitten, which her clinic dubbed Squash, little did we know he would be our new dog.

We had only lived in Raleigh, North Carolina a short time when the kitten came into our lives. As former firefighters in a small town in central New Hampshire, the time had come to seek another home with less snow and more sunshine. We'd barely settled in to our gray ranch and had planned to adopt a pet anyway. So, the kitten stayed. We had thought about getting a dog, but my sister had a lovely golden retriever that needed watching while she worked. Besides, ever since I was a very small child, I have always had a cat in our home. Cats have a calming effect on me, whether I had a tough test at school, a harrowing call as a 9-1-1 dispatcher, or a depressing day as a writer where nothing went right. My cat's purring seemed to say, "Be happy."

As we transitioned to 'empty nesters', a low-maintenance kitten made perfect sense. However, the late John Lennon said, "Life is what happens when you are busy making other plans." I discovered that this kitten planned to rule his world. From the start, the kitten told the dog he was in charge.   Poor Hilary would go out of her way not to walk by the little puff of tiger-striped fur. With the slash of white down his nose, and our history as firefighters, we renamed him Blaze.

Blaze acts more like a dog than a cat, such as when he stretches out in front of the fireplace. I started saying, "Roll over" on a whim, and he rolled over. He still reacts that way, about 50% of the time. Yes, he's a cat. I don't do everything I'm told, either.

At bedtime, after walking in circles, Blaze settles on the blanket, at the foot of our bed, but only on my husband's side. When hubby comes to bed, Blaze jumps off and disappears.   During colder months, we wake to find Blaze squeezed between us, reminding me of our two sons as children. Sleep in? Not possible if Blaze is hungry.

In the morning, when I get out of bed, he precedes me to my bathroom. When I shower, he either waits for me on the closed toilet seat, or sits outside my curtain with his back to me. When I peek at him from behind the shower curtain, he looks up at me and meows, as if saying, "Look at what a good job I'm doing, protecting you!"

Later in the day, if I head to the bathroom or bedroom, and ask, "You com'n?" he runs at full gallop past me. If I am working in my office, he head-bashes the partially closed door, and jumps on the desk nearest the window. If the door is closed, he scratches on it until I cringe at the sound and open it. I wish he would learn to close the door. When I turn on the shredder, he sniffs it, then ignores it. Loud sounds do not seem to bother him, unless I pull out the vacuum cleaner. Both Blaze and Hilary would immediately run away. I presume loud things that move are to be avoided at all costs. A practical lesson.

When he jumps up on the stereo and rubs against a large framed painting, I worry he will bring it down upon his head. If I want him elsewhere, all I have to do is say 'git' and he runs. Oh, he isn't a coward. Nope, not Blaze. If a car door slams, or a delivery truck stops anywhere near our house, Blaze's ears perk up, and he growls. I keep expecting him to bark. If the person coming through the door is my husband, Blaze jumps onto a chair or table and head-butts him in welcome.

As a writer, I sometimes like to sit at the dining room table where I can spread out. Blaze has to sit on something on the table…a notebook, folder, thick binder, or even my power

174

cord. At times, he looks uncomfortable, but that's Blaze. He is very photogenic and I share photos of him acting as my muse on social media.

My youngest son travels for work, but when he is able to stop
by, I say to Blaze, "He's coming, your boy!" The cat's ears twitch, and he watches out the window until my son arrives, then rolls around the floor with him. Playing with him is fine, but don't try to pick him up. Nope, not going there. I do it only when necessary, because he goes all stiff. I worry the people who had him for his first four months of life mistreated him, and it breaks my heart that he might remember. He makes me do my best to be kind to others. A lesson we should all live by.

At meal times, he sits behind his bowl and watches us prepare our food. If we look like we might sit down and eat without filling his bowl, he meows. Loudly. When we fill his bowl, he eats some, then leaves the rest as if to say, "Just wanted to make sure I got mine." I put him on a diet after he tipped the scales over fifteen pounds, but he seems fine with the smaller measured portions. I wish I could lose weight, too. Hmmm, maybe there is another lesson, there.

Dogs like to play, but Blaze plays like no cat I've ever seen. If he runs into the bedroom with me, he sometimes disappears behind a floor-to-ceiling curtain. I say "Where's the kitty?" and the curtain moves as he races end to end. If I sneak up on him, and peek, he will either play-attack me, or meow. It is times like this when I miss playing games with my two little boys.

Blaze can be skittish. One year during TV's Shark Week I started yelling "Shark!" and threw a pencil onto the floor near him, and he ran. I did it several times over the course of the week. Now if I yell "Shark!" he still runs

175

away! (Let's be truthful. If someone yelled that at me, I'd be outta here!) Blaze sits on my lap, the way my children did. Love washes over me each time, realizing this tiny creature loves me and might actually need me.

Many years have passed since my sister asked us to watch a sweet little kitten while their clinic tried to find him a home. Ever since Blaze came into our lives, he keeps me company while I work at home on my writing. Dear Hilary died of cancer, and the memories of previous cats in my life fills me with dread each time Blaze acts ill. I take comfort in watching over him, the same way I watched over my sons. After all, he makes our 'nest' feel less empty. It only took a day to know Blaze was our kind of dog…I mean, cat.

Nancy Lee Badger

Arlene S. Bice is author of non-fiction books on local history, metaphysics, hauntings, memoir, poetry, and is published in many anthologies. She is a member of TAF, IWWG, NFAA, and WAM.

Deep in the Forest

My friend Kevin, who knows me well, asked me to accompany him to see something he found deep in the forest. Hmm. I love the forest, so why not?

We arrived on a pleasantly warm, sunny, early autumn afternoon. After parking the car, we walked quite a while on a wide dirt path. It narrowed to single file before Kevin stepped onto a path trodden over grass and weeds. He seemed to know where he was going. When we reached a large clearing in the middle of dense trees, he stopped. His right hand slipped around mine and he pointed with his left.

"Look, do you see that?" he pointed to a row of roughly cut logs, laying inches from each other, approximately 8' in length.

"How curious," I said, not to make a fuss about it. "Maybe it's a logging company that is coming back for them?"

He looked at me curiously. "There are no truck tire marks, tracks, or planks set down as they do when they are clearing a forest. Come over here." He led me just a few feet beyond to another wide row of logs laid out in the same way. His eyes bored into mine as he waited for a surprised reply. No reply came from me.

177

"No stopping now. There is more, look." We moved down another 50 feet. Yep. A replay of the earlier logs. This time he lifted the end of one log to reveal a shallow grave with what appeared to be a young man's body looking peaceful with his hands crossed on his chest. He didn't appear to have been there very long as his body had not deteriorated. "I received an anonymous phone call," he said.

"Well, we are here," I said quietly as I looked rather calmly, maybe lovingly at the body. "I brought a picnic basket when you said we were going into the forest. Let's find a comfortable spot and I'll let you in on a wee secret." Stunned! He was absolutely stunned! His mouth dropped open! He expected to shock or at least un-nerve me! Instead the opposite happened!
He stammered. "F-F-Food? You want me to eat after seeing this dead body? I lifted many of the logs to reveal other bodies! This is sinister, evil, and dreadfully wrong! And you want to feed me?"

"You know I always like to feed my friends and things are not always what they appear to be." I told him to take a deep breath, actually a couple deep breaths. He always trusted me and I knew my dear friend would trust me now.

"Let's back-track to a favorite picnic spot of mine. It's a good distance away from this area." I continued.

Neither of us spoke a word as we walked back and unloaded the car. I wondered what was going through his mind. We settled in the sunshine near the lake on a blanket I'd brought. The water sparkled, birds chirped, trees whispered gently as they dropped their colorful leaves. The aroma of wood burning a far distance away floated in the air. The quiet of the forest was soothing.

I unpacked the lunch basket; spread out bowls of cold, crispy, fried chicken, Deviled Eggs made with spicy brown mustard, mayo, and Boursin cheese; chips, bleu cheese dip, blueberry hand pies for dessert, and a bottle of chilled Sauvignon Blanc wine. Wine was good for easing rough edges. Kevin opened it expertly, filling two glasses quickly and gulping his down before he reached for a piece of chicken.

So much for being too upset to eat, I thought. With glass in hand, I began. "I think you've met my friend Dr. Watson." I went on to explain how a year ago he brought me into the forest with some background information of a complex problem he wanted to discuss with me. At first he was a bit concerned about how I would react after stepping into this strange situation without warning.

"You know I consider him weird, but he is your friend so I give him a certain amount of respect." That was Kevin's only comment so far. I still had his full attention, other than the chicken, that is. I picked up where I left off.

"There were no logs here then, only people, young people in their early 20s through late 30s. They were a nice group and at first I couldn't figure why Dr. Watson, Craig as I call him, invited me. Little by little I realized they were not what we considered a normal group."

Kevin knew my penchant for studying people. He never responded to my intense scrutiny of their faces without appearing to stare. He knew how I did that as a writer does, observing human nature.

"A few had slight eruptions on their faces. I noticed it on the hands of a couple others."

I watched Kevin's green eyes widen in anticipation. I half expected his black curls to stand on end. A touch of

179

gray appeared at the temples. Strange, to notice that now, at this time.

"Craig introduced me to Marc, a handsome fellow, physically fit like a man who doesn't sit in front of a TV every night eating Whoppers or Supersize anything. I took a liking to him immediately."

In our many discussions, Kevin and I acknowledged that odd pull of a like-minded person. Marc had that interesting demeanor. While he was talking I noticed an area alongside of his nose that looked like a puffy mole.

"Marc led me over to meet Paul his closest friend. The backs of both Paul's hands were erupted to the size of a 50-cent coin. It was definitely noticeable. I'm sure they saw me take note though I purposely kept my facial expressions neutral."

"What was it? Was it contagious? Why would Watson take you to such a place? Damn the man!" Kevin's alarm was sincere and not unexpected.

"Easy, Kevin. You know Craig well enough to know he would never intentionally endanger my life or health. He knew I would want to help this group if I could. They were all non-contagious."

I went on to explain that it was some modern, rare strain of an incurable, unstoppable disease. There presently was nothing that could be done to help these bright, young people who had so much to contribute to the world.

As we discussed the problem, I knew that I would be part of a team to help where I could.

"At one point I looked up to see a lovely, young lady enter the cleared circle with an air of elegance, unexpected so deep in the forest. Marc quietly confided to me that she was a leading, internationally known fashion model. This

180

disease had ended her career. She offered her body to the medical field to end her life now and use it for science research with the idea of perhaps saving a future generation. She felt that her life became useless, unlivable without her role as a model."

I went on to tell Kevin that before the end of the day, I had decided to help, just not sure how. I had talked with many of the group. Several of them closely connected with me, touching me deeply. We came up with a plan, not able to stop the disease from progressing, but something else to help in a some way.

It was time for me to pause, sip some wine and nibble a bit while Kevin absorbed all that I revealed so far. I calmly waited for his questions before I went any further because I would need his help with this project. He was not only my dear friend, but also my publisher.

"Okay, I'll bite. You brought me lunch for a reason. What is it? C'mon. You can tell me, or should I say, ask me?" He was grinning so I sensed the time was right.

"Well, since you mentioned it…wait. Let me tell you more, first. I went home and thought about this brave assortment of people who shared the same obstacle in life. Youth is deeply impressed with looks and appearance, especially about themselves."

Kevin listened closely to Part One of my plan. My calendar was cleared to devote my time with only them. I took a professional photo of every person while they were still handsome and lovely, tipping the camera away from any eruptions on their faces. I spent private time with each one to write their story and the words they wanted to leave after they were gone. I found them to be smart, sensitive and caring. It's horrible. This disease truly disfigures them to disturbingly ugly. It will also cruelly change them inside as they age.

"It took months to complete, working intensely. I wasn't sure exactly what I would do with it. This assembly of people matter. What do you think?"

"I think it would have been better if you called me in on this sooner. It's something that I could have been part of; contributed to."

"Of course I thought of you as I tossed, turned, and struggled, trying to sleep; seeking answers. You were in Europe, out of touch. I tried to call you and even had your office, against their better judgement, try to reach you. Of course I wanted you in on this."

"I do apologize for that snip of attitude. I was on a hush-hush government project. I couldn't tell you about it, either. I was away much longer than expected. I apologize. I am interested as I think you knew I would be. What have you come up with?"

"Everyone in this group agreed that living life with this new, modern strain of disease was not worth living. They believed they could make an impact if they ended their lives as a collective to bring international attention to their medical dilemma."

He remained quiet about the next part of the plan, to publish a book and publicize it big time.

"It's imperative that their faces become familiar in every country, by everyone i.e. like Steve McCurry's 1984 photo of the orphan, 'Afghan Girl' with her piercing green eyes that became the cover of National Geographic.

"Their names will go down in history. The medical field must be drawn to this terrible disease and eradicate it before it ruins the lives of another generation of young people. The world must not wait too long as it did with HIV/AIDS before it is curbed."

Again I paused for effect, letting the enormity of it sink in. "You are the best there is at publishing and promotion. Your help is desperately needed."

It was then that I pulled the box stuffed with 8" x 12" brown envelopes out of the back of the car. Forty envelopes for Kevin to open, study the photo, and read the life story within. These were copies to take with him. I had a set and I gave Craig a set as soon as I finished them.

"There is more to tell you. Let's finish the last of the wine while it is still cool.

"When I finished recording all there was to record, the group had made a decision. They, each one, signed a pact. They would end their life now. They did. Now was ten months ago."

"Ten months ago! That can't be! The bodies I saw look like they have only been there for a day or two!"

"I know. That, I believe will be part of this entire puzzle. Their bodies have not been touched by any chemical or any special liquid. As they died, so they lay. I did not ask how they died. I do not want to know nor do I want to incriminate anyone who had a hand it in. That is not part of my responsibility."

It would be noted that this group of young people had surely given up their lives to save the world as well as any military person who lost a life in battle. Their battle was of a different kind, yet just as devastating, if this battle was not ended.

"I schooled them on what I know about life-after-life from my own personal experiences. Plus I gave them sources of information to read, watch, and listen. Their final decision was one full of knowledge and of course, a personal one. I spoke one on one with each and found contentment and peace."

Kevin smiled as he read my side notes. (A great deal of time and focus was spent with a select handful that I became close to. We have arranged many particular communications i.e. omens, words, scents, even apparitions if they have that power after they have passed beyond the veil. Some spirits seem to have that power in the afterlife and others do not. I have yet to learn why.)

"To date, I have received messages from 6 out of the 10 that agreed to contact me. Marc is the only one that has actually appeared before me. He was the one I expected to hear from first, because we truly connected with each other. I'm thinking that we had a close friendship in a past life. In time I will pursue that but I don't want it to interfere with this project. I only saw his face. It was grinning from side to side without a blemish on it. There is no denying he made the right choice. For others appearing can take any amount of earthly time.

"I'm happy to report that all the messages are uplifting responses. One even wrote a happy face on the steamy mirror in my bathroom. I was deliriously happy in return, laughing out loud at 6 a.m.!"

Kevin reached out and took my hand. "You have amazed me from the first time we met." He said "and you continue to amaze me. There is no end to your wonder."

I could only smile at him extending that invisible bond that connected us. He would stand with me on this project as he had in many others.

"Here is the updated report Craig sent. I have no contact with the scientists. They are working on finding the cure and the reason why their bodies have not deteriorated as a body normally would do. It may be connected to the disease. They are a devoted bunch, wholly on board. A few of them even believe in the afterlife!"

"That's saying something for a scientist. I wonder if any of them has had a personal experience." Kevin said.

"Well," Kevin continued, releasing my hand and patting his full stomach. "I'm on board. We will publish the book and give it top notch push. Prepare for a full book tour, appearances on TV shows, the whole works. This is going to be the big one that gets everyone's attention! We'll blow the world out of the water! Be prepared for the naysayers. There will also be a fight ahead of us. It may get nasty, but I'm with you."

I packed up what little was left of lunch. Empty containers and an empty wine bottle was the distinct message that lunch was as good as the conversation. No spirits needed to appear for confirmation on that!

Arlene S. Bice

*"The most powerful person in the world is the storyteller.
The storyteller sets the vision, values and agenda of an entire generation that is to come."*

\- Steve Jobs

Our Writers. . .

Nancy Lee Badger is an award-winning, multi-published author who grew up in New York State. She was an EMT and volunteer firefighter and retired from a nearly 10-year 911 Dispatcher in New Hampshire before moving to Raleigh, NC where she writes stories with a twist. She is a member of TAF, RWA, HCRW, and Fantasy-Futuristic & Paranormal Romance Writers.

Lois Thompson Bartholomew made her first writing sale in 1979, a parenting tip that sold for $10. Houghton Mifflin Harcourt bought her first novel The White Dove. It is republished as an Ebook, a paperback, and an audiobook available at books2read.com/ltbart and https://shop.authors-direct.com and https://www.loisthompsonbartholomew.com/ She is a member of SCBWI and TAF.

Drew Becker is a multi-book author, poet, writing coach, branding architect, and publisher at Realization Press (RealizationPress.com). His recent book, The Joyful Brand: Personal Branding for Authors, Speakers and the Rest of Us, includes exercises to help define personal brands. He collaborates with authors to help them publish and prosper.

Arlene S Bice is author of non-fiction books on local history, metaphysics, hauntings, memoir, poetry, and is published in many anthologies. She is a member of TAF, IWWG, NFAA, and Co-Founding member of WAM. Her books are available at Oakley Hall Antiques & Art in Warrenton (NC). Website: http://arlenebice.com/

P.J. Black is the author of Selene Darke Series. Book One: Almost Darke. Book Two is due out in 2022. He is a gamer and avid science fiction/fantasy fan who enjoys anime, erotica, humor, and martial arts movies. This happens under the supervision of his four black cats. His books are in ebook and paperback form.

Patricia "Pat" Bumpass is author of Jump into Creativity, a freelance content creator for small businesses, and coach who encourages and empowers women of color to lean into their true authentic selves by engaging in self-care. She is the creator of beautiful, motivational 44-card decks that inspire. They're great for women writers! Learn more at www.patriciabumpass.com

Barbara Burns, Ph.D. is a published writer, educator, naturalist, and retired psychologist. She is a graduate of Rice University, a doctorate from U. Missouri, and a Master's from U. Tennessee. She is a past member of Southern Highland Craft Guild and a member of TAF. Her activities include researching, writing, painting, fossil hunting, and birding.

Lauren Clemmons is a published author based in Raleigh, North Carolina. Her essays, poetry, and fiction appear in anthologies, including TAF publications.

Rebecca Dalton has been reading science fiction since she was a kid and her mom introduced her to it. She writes stories that explore what our future could look like, and all the ways that people can make the world better by working together. Visit her at RebeccaDalton.net.

Marvis Henderson-Daye has published her debut novel, Nine Lives and a nonfiction ebook, Every Storm Runs out of Rain. She is CEO of M. E. Henderson, Inc. where she uses urban line dancing to create a healthy community. She is a member of Triangle Association of Freelancers.

Erika V. Hoffman's fiction was publ. in Deadly Ink Anthologies, Tough Lit. Magazine, and Page & Spine and Why Mama after it won First Place in a contest. Erika's stories appear in Chicken Soup for the Soul and Sasee among other publications. Her published stories are formatted into books.

Terri DeGezelle Michels, author and photographer, has published more than 60 children's non-fiction titles. Her newest title, Simon of Cyrene, the Legend of the Easter Egg published by Pauline Books and Media. Terri shares her writing experiences during school visits, encouraging children to follow their dream.

K Ann Pennington is a social studies teacher who has traveled over 30,000 miles around the United States by RV. Pastimes include examining primary source materials and performing field research, especially on the Civil War. She is working on an historical novel that takes place on the Rocky Mountain frontier just after the Civil War.

Sarah Merritt Ryan is a published academic, a commercial blogger, and has poetry published in Hope Whispers, Whispering Angels Books. She is a Triangle, North Carolina native who has a lifelong passion for creative writing through poetry and creative nonfiction. Her creative spark is found through nature, people, and reflection.

Ana Shapkaliska is a scriptwriter, novelist, and short story writer from North Macedonia. Many of her TV projects in Europe won awards at European TV Festivals. Her novel

"Govinda, Anuttam and the Juhu Temple" was published by TRI. She lives with her husband in Cary, North Carolina. www.anashapkaliska.com

Don Vaughan has made his living with words for more than four decades. His work has appeared in an eclectic array of markets, including Writer's Digest, MAD Magazine, Encyclopedia Britannica, Military Officer Magazine and Sky & Telescope. Don is the founder of Triangle Association of Freelancers (tafnc.com).

Edward Wills is a writer living in Eastern North Carolina. Formerly, he was a reporter at three Midwestern newspapers, a magazine editor, and a non-profit executive.

Chanah Wizenberg received her BA from Hunter College in English and Creative Writing. Her writing has appeared in several magazines and multiple anthologies. Chanah has been a professional ballerina, a pastry chef, and English teacher. She resides in Raleigh, North Carolina with her dog, Asha, and her cat, Marmalade.

About the Editor

Arlene S. Bice is an author of more than a dozen non-fiction books on New Jersey history, memoir, metaphysics, poetry, and published in multiple anthologies. She assists others in independent publishing and has led writing groups since 1998. Pre-pandemic Bice hosted Sunday Poetry in Nature afternoons in the garden at Backyard Birds and Rosemont Vineyards. She led writing workshops on Memoir.

Her poems *A Writer's Pandemic* and *New Orleans* were performed in the Pandemic Blues at the Kirby Theatre directed by Fred Motley in Roxboro, North Carolina. She is an award-winning artist.

Bice is the former proprietor of By the Book @ U & I Gift Shop for nearly 20 years and wrote a book review column for the Register-News for 10 years. She holds memberships in Triangle Association of Freelancers (TAF), Nonfiction Authors Association (NFAA), International Women's Writing Guild (IWWG), and is a founding member of the Warren Artists Market (WAM). She lives in Virginia with her bossy, black cat Captain Midnight.
Website: arlenebice.com

Acknowledgements

Thank you to the TAF Board of Directors for their belief, encouragement and guidelines.
Thank you to Rebecca Dalton for taking the responsibility to secure a great cover and printing.
Thank you to each TAF member
Thank you to each writer who stepped out of their usual writing genre to explore and submit fiction.

A premature *thank you* to everyone who enjoys reading our TAF Omnibus.